KIDNAP, ROB
THEN IT ALL WENT....

Jack Trichaud only wanted a quiet life in small town Ohio. But when you're in possession of nearly a million dollars from a bank robbery gone wrong, life is anything but quiet.

On the one hand, Agent Pippin is searching for the evidence that will pin the robbery on Jack and send him away for a good long time. On the other hand, violent White Power thug Calderone – aided by his merciless girlfriend and Jack's own long lost brother – wants the money and he doesn't care who he has to hurt to get it. In fact, the more pain Jack suffers the happier Calderone will be.

Jack has more than a few cards up his sleeve, but blood will be spilled and he's going to need every trick in the book to make sure it's not his.

Or not too much of it, anyway.

PRAISE FOR ROBERT WHITE

"Explosive pulp action from start to finish...Brutal and unrelenting, *When You Run with Wolves* is written with a rare intelligence and wit that almost belies its violent heart." -Michael Young, author of *All Blood is Red* and *Of Blondes and Bullets*

"Grabs you by the soul and doesn't let go!" -Simon Woods, author of *The Fall Guy*

"White writes beautiful, wrenching prose. *Haftmann's Rules* is stark and unsentimental. It's White at his best." -Cindy Rosmus, author & publisher of Yellow Mama

"White's stories are gritty and intense." -Douglas Rhodes, editor, Sex and Murder Magazine

"Robert White knows the subconscious well and tells an immensely gripping tale on numerous levels!" -*HorrorNews.net*

"[White's characters] are experiencing the ultimate horror of being deeply alone. Yet there is more to the collection than its abandoned characters; it is also the subtle workings of White's hard-boiled style that often lures the reader into experiencing the same loneliness." -Joe Zingaro

#4

WHEN YOU RUN WITH WOLVES

ROBERT WHITE

#13 Press

ntp-13A04

\#

Copyright Robert White, 2015
Cover design copyright Number Thirteen Press, 2015

All characters and events are fictitious. Any resemblance to actual events or persons, living or dead, is entirely coincidental.

All rights reserved.

Published by Number Thirteen Press

\#

#

FOR LINDY LINDELL

#

You can choose many things in this life, but you can't pick the egg and sperm that designed you. My brother and I were lucky in one respect because our mother lived long enough to insist to our father that he not name us Castor and Pollux as he had informed her many times he had every intention of doing. I have no memory of her but it must have been one of the few times she ever stood up to him. He wasn't an easy man to live with.

My mother disappeared from my life when my brother was born. She died of an infection contracted in the hospital. My father later told me I walked around our Montreal apartment muttering "no-so-com-i-al" for days afterward. I must have overheard him talking to the doctor on the phone. But I don't remember. I remember that my father was proud I knew such a big word at my young age. He would become much prouder of my younger brother. Carlos not only looked like him with his wheat-colored hair and ice-blue eyes, but also had my father's gift for languages.

For years after my mother's death, my brother and I sat at the supper table learning various tongues in a kind of surcharged Berlioz. My father told us these were replicas of the same courses he himself had taken for his assignments abroad. My brother responded to my father's prompts with a mastery I never could attain. I carry around a sharp memory of them carrying on an intense conversation in German. I could barely follow, missing every other word as if those pesky irregular verbs were vines tripping me up.

What I didn't learn until years later is that we weren't speaking German at all, just a pidgin form of it my father learned and taught from flashcards he had bought in some decrepit bookshop in Old Montreal. In fact, the only language we did pick up was a smattering of Quebeçois French – and that mostly obscenities – from hanging around with older boys down by the river. My father said he worked for the C.I.A., but when he left the house it was for menial jobs like short-order cook, shoe salesman, a glassware plant on the St. Lawrence. These, he said, were his "cover" while on assignment. My brother and I believed him. Maybe you would have too.

My father disappeared from our lives forever on August 22, although I'm never sure if it was 1988 or 1989. The date I recall because it is on August 22 that the last Imam disappeared and will reappear. It's also the day in 1187 when Saladdin conquered Jerusalem. Our father loved trivia like that.

My memory of him the week before he flew the coop is vague like so much else in the intervening years. He must have been preparing to leave, but I don't recall that he acted any differently. He treated my brother and me the same, except that he wasn't talking to himself so much as muttering or making comments to an invisible audience. It sticks in my mind for some reason that he quoted Réne Levèsque: 'There are moments when courage and daring are the only acceptable forms of caution.'

I still have a fuzzy recollection of him walking from room to room in our small flat. He was moving things around, looking for something, maybe a passport, setting stacks of books aside where they had been growing upwards like models of multicolored skyscrapers, each with a patina of dust on whichever book had been added last. He rummaged among files (his 'declassified' ones) we had been ordered never to disturb. He was muttering to himself in his unique polyglot of Russian, Pashtun (he said), and Creole, which he claimed to have picked up years before during a posting in the Lesser Antilles before he met my mother.

My brother learned how to use a computer during his time in Dannemora for armed robbery. I'm not surprised he never bothered to try to locate the old man. He had it much worse. When I ran off at seventeen, he had our father all to himself. But this is not a story about our running father or a prodigal son. It's a story of what happened two weeks after my brother discovered I was living in Northtown, Ohio, a quiet, working-class burg on the shores of Lake Erie…

TUESDAY, SEPTEMBER 7

7:05 A.M.

#1

The cops walked in while I was drinking coffee in a rumpsprung wicker chair on my back porch. Chickadees and yard sparrows darted in and out of the big Rose-of-Sharon bush by the fence out back.

I had just come out of the deepest sleep I can remember in months. I remember only a tiny part of the last dream: I was climbing a huge pole with iron rungs, high up into the clouds. I was delivering mail bags for the airplanes, which would fly past and catch them by their tailhooks. Jack and the Beanstalk – except this Jack was returning the bags.

Five of them, to be precise. Moneybags. All stolen from the Fifth Third Bank of Northtown, Ohio. A place I had called home for the last ten years of my life until my ex-con brother and Randall J. Calderone showed up at my doorstep and insisted I help them rob it.

For his own amusement, the Roller of Dice in the Sky carves out a few of his subjects for a special kind of mockery. My brother's criminal life was proof enough. Many times my brother Carlos and I would regret that our father wasn't your average kind of nut who believes in little green space aliens. My father's dementia kept his past a secret from us and our mother back in Montreal. He had that kind of knowledge so that, if you tried to discover anything about who he was or where he came from, he'd be there to confront you, and the last thing you wanted was to get caught spying on a spy who was acutely paranoid. I don't know that he would have turned on us and killed us in our beds, but it was a thought that justified my desertion.

I asked the detectives if I was under arrest and one said "not at this time" but my cooperation would be "appreciated." The man in charge was short and squat, fair-complected, had thin sandy hair in fast retreat, and a nose full of busted capillaries that showed he liked a drink now and then. He said he was a Special Investigator from the BCI in Columbus. He didn't look as if he expected to be disappointed by my refusal to cooperate.

The cop who opened the cruiser door for me said, "Watch your head" out of habit. It was one of those unmarked ones in front of the street and had old food smells in it. I was surprised that I didn't have much appetite and wondered about my lack of interest in eating. I moved my belt over another notch that morning, which made three in the last ten days. My body still trusted me even if, lately, my mind wasn't so sure about things.

If it weren't for the cop cars all over the parking lot, you'd think it was a small-town library. I asked one officer if the lineup was supposed to take a long time. He said he didn't know because he was using the facility courtesy of the locals. He didn't want to inconvenience me by driving all the way to Lake County. Normally, he said, they did this kind of thing with photos. They took me into a side door beneath the main reception center. A few cops and dispatchers were chatting and drinking coffee. No one paid me any attention. A cop put me in a small interview room and asked me to wait there for a few minutes. He said he had to get some information from me before they could start the lineup. He asked me if I wanted any coffee, and I said no thanks.

He shut the door and left me there. The room, like the building, was new. I remembered the groundbreaking ceremony in the paper, and the blond wood had a wax shine to it. There wasn't any desperate graffiti scratched into the walls or the wood surface. It felt like waiting to be summoned for a job interview. The only thing that gave the room a Mickey Spillane feel was the small mirror opposite me. I sat there for ten minutes before the BCI investigator and a detective named Narducci came in. A nattily dressed, tall black man who identified himself as Agent Pippin of the FBI entered last and closed the door behind him. It wasn't just his haberdashery that impressed me. He had an air about him that said he was alpha male in this room. It was Narducci, however, who apologized for the delay. They were having a little trouble with the arrangements this morning, he said, "just one of those things," but he expected to get it fixed soon. He was sorry and asked me again if I wanted any coffee and I said no. He said he didn't blame me. It was the worst coffee he had ever had except for what his wife made. I smiled, all three left the room, and I sat there for another twenty minutes. I heard noises from time to time beyond the door but nothing distinguishable.

Det. Narducci, looking flustered, came back alone this time. He had a form he said he needed to fill out for their records and asked me some questions – my name, and age, and how long I lived in town. Where I went to school, and my last place of employment. He wrote everything down and then said a detective would be coming to get me very soon.

Instead the BCI investigator came back, his face was flushed and he was out of breath. He told me the lineup was canceled and he apologized again for wasting my time. He said an officer would drive me back to my house.

Somehow, I wasn't surprised to see Agent Pippin himself sitting on my front porch. He was as nattily dressed as before but this time it was a navy blue pinstripe suit with a powder blue shirt and red tie. He liked to make a good second impression. He smiled at me as the officer opened the door for us.

"You're coming up in the world, Jack," he said. "Chauffeured service right to your doorstep, my-oh-my."

"What do you want, Agent Pippin?"

"Oh, let's see, just a few minutes of your time."

"You had an hour of staring at me through a two-way mirror. Isn't that enough for you?"

I had no doubt it was he who had arranged that little dog-and-pony show back at the station. I walked past him but he followed me right through the open doorway.

I walked into the kitchen and drank some water from the tap.

"That's one of the major causes of germ spreading, Jack. If you were to see some microscopic slides of what's on one of those grotty faucets, you'd never do that again."

"Don't you have to be invited into a person's house before you're permitted to interrogate them?" I said.

"You're thinking of Satan," he said. "The soul has to succumb before the devil may be permitted to walk in, so to speak."

"You're a theologian, too," I said.

"Just a Roman Catholic," he said. "Do you believe in God?"

"No," I said. "I refuse to believe in any intelligent designer who isn't himself an out-and-out maniac. Only a sadist could have made a cesspool of a world like this."

"You're confusing creationism with Darwinian evolution, Jack."

"Am I?"

"Faith is about belief. Belief in goodness, in the immortality of the soul, in life everlasting."

"By your terms, then, I have no faith," I said.

"That's a pity," he said. "It means you have nothing to look forward to."

"That's right. Good old nothingness. The inanimate, eternal void."

"How did you do it? Just tell me that much and I'll go."

"Do what?"

"Every one of them picked your brother and Calderone out of the photo lineup before I got done putting them down on the table. But none of the family could positively identify you. They didn't recognize you without that nylon stocking you wore and they didn't remember ever hearing you speak above a whisper in the house the whole day they were held captive." Pippin laughed. "I've never seen anything like it."

"Isn't there a lot of literature in your field about the unreliability of eyewitness identification?"

He leaned against my kitchen counter and rested a hand on his hip. He glittered with gold accoutrement. I remembered a waterlogged paperback of old poems my father once brought home. One was about a man who glittered when he walked. He committed suicide.

"Your size, your build, your hair color. But nobody could agree on how you walked or how deep your voice was." He jabbed a finger at my chest. "You are the third man, Trichaud – if that's even your name."

I shrugged and walked out to the porch. I saw a ruby-throated hummingbird at the feeder. I wondered how much more life it packed into a second than a human being.

"Then prove it," I said. I thought he was going to hit me right then and there.

"Oh, I'll prove it, all right. Don't you worry about that, Perry fucking Mason."

"Maybe you should be out looking for Calderone," I said.

"We'll get them. We've got choppers coming up from Columbus with heat-seeking and infrared cameras. The dogs'll track them before then or they'll come stumbling out the woods full of ticks. They do what boneheads like them on the run always do."

"Best of luck, Agent Pippin."

"These local cops underestimate you. That BCI agent with the cheap cologne thinks you'll roll over on your brother and Calderone as soon as we bag them. He says you're just some pussy landscaper, not a master criminal lured into a heist by his convict brother and a real bad ass.

"I consider Carlos more a sibling than a brother," I said. "We're not close."

"What was your father thinking, giving him a Mex name?"

"You're a black man and you ask me about non-Caucasian kids' names?"

"Racist," said Pippin.

"You mean 'bigot,' don't you?"

"Whatever, if the shoe or the shit fits, Trichaud."

"No, not really. I just know what it's like to be a foreigner and have kids gang up on you because you aren't one of them."

"Speaking of your past, I got a question for you. I checked you out. I go back ten years and you disappear from the databases. Why is that, Trichaud? There's no paper on you older than ten years."

"It must have burned in a fire."

"I'd say that's a lot of fires in a lot of record departments."

"Is that illegal?"

"Robbing banks is illegal, Jack. Kidnapping and holding hostages, terrorist threats – why, those are illegal, believe it or not. Strapping a live bomb to her husband's back – that's really illegal. The penal code frowns on such activities among its citizenry. You do what we call 'the hard forty' for that stuff in Ohio, Jack."

"Why tell me, Agent Pippin?"

"The bomb disposal unit said that thing should have gone off in something like ten seconds and there was enough Semtec to knock the whole structure of the house down."

My knees wobbled. I hadn't thought my brother capable of anything like that. But he had to be the designer of the bomb. That moron he showed up with couldn't pour piss out of a boot with the directions on the heel.

"Now why would anyone build a bomb that sophisticated, arm it, and then shut it down?"

"You really should find this Calderone if you want an answer to that one," I said.

"Yeah, I forgot. You just plant flowers. That's what the cops here can't understand. Calderone and your brother didn't bother to disguise themselves. Your brother's quite the chatterbox, though. He talked and smoked dope all night long. They didn't care about those people's lives, Jack. That little girl. Her boyfriend, the father – all of them could've been vaporized for five bags of money. Makes you feel proud, doesn't it? To be the brother of a lowlife worm who can take life so easily."

"You'll have to ask my brother that one," I said.

"Oh I will. Be sure of that. Just before we throw the key away on his worthless ass, I'll be sure to write down his answer to that one. I don't know how you got round that woman. I don't know what you did or said to her that she won't identify you when she was close enough to spit into your eye. But I am going to make that question the focus of my life's work from now on."

"It's good to have a hobby. Now if you'll pardon me, I've got some birds to watch."

My back was turned, but I felt him breathing behind me. In truth, I wasn't trying to get his goat. I just wanted him gone to think. Alicia Fox-Whitcomb was bank manager of the Fifth Third and the woman we terrorized until she cooperated and got us into the bank vault. But Ms. Fox-Whitcomb's refusal to identify me back at the station wasn't a gift I could take advantage of forever – not with Calderone waiting for my call in a couple hours. I never doubted for a second he had more cunning than to get himself caught stumbling around lost in the woods or boosting a car. My brother might have done the planning, but he was nothing more than a pilot fish to this shark.

My father in his delusional 'Soviet phase' as a CIA spy used to quote Russian proverbs. One came to mind: The groundhog knows many things. But the fox knows one thing.

#2

The phone rang at twenty-five to noon.

"Jack, are you going to be out of there?"

"I want to see you, Sarah." My not-quite-yet-divorced ex.

"Don't be stupid, Jack. We're past that now."

"I'm not past it, Sarah. I don't want to be past it," I said.

There was a long pause. "It's too late," she said. "It's over, Jack."

God Almighty, I was hearing soap opera dialogue in what was the collapsing building of my life; before I knew it, this came out of my mouth: "I can change things," I said.

Both expected and lame. "No, you can't. I haven't got the rest of my life to wait even if I thought that was the truth. You've been half there for years."

"I had to work, didn't I?"

"I'm talking about another kind of thereness," she said.

Now we were shifting into TV shrink speech. "Is that why you cheated? Did I just imagine your new stud on his shiny motorcycle?"

"It's not going to get us anywhere if we start making recriminations about who did what to whom," she said. I knew that tone well.

"Why is it that when people are caught rutting in the mud like pigs, the language suddenly elevates to fine words like 'recriminations' and 'whom'?"

"I want to know if you're going to be out of the house by tomorrow afternoon. I have some contractors and painters coming over at one o'clock."

"Goodbye, Sarah."

#3

I needed a shower and a shave. I was just turning the corner of the stairs when the phone rang again.

"Sarah, I don't have time for this right now-"

"Who's Sarah?" Marija asked.

Her laugh was a jolt of adrenalin straight into my stomach. An image of her sent the blood rushing south like one of those Californian mud slides. Here I was moping over one woman and two seconds later lusting for a different one. The first time I saw Marija Ercegovic she said she was on vacation in America. She laughed at my pronunciation of her name.

I thought from her accented English she was

Hungarian. I even had a flashback to one of the old man's lessons in a goofy version of Magyar at that other kitchen table. She was from Dubrovnic on the Adriatic coast. She had a large family there, she said. My father's dog-eared Atlas popped into my head. Carlos and I had fought over it so often that its spine was cracked and frayed. We used to hide it from each other. Ancient and badly outdated, at least a dozen East European and Central Asian countries weren't called by their right names. My father insisted we learn their vital statistics, culture, demographics, and important historical dates. Carlos soaked up information like a blotter and could recite principal imports and exports, GNPs, and other kinds of trivia back at my father whereas I stumbled through these recitations. My father used to shake his head in dismay. He had the field agent's contempt for desk jockeys. It took me years to unlearn some of it, but by then I had acquired a way to compartmentalize much of the tangle of lies my old man created.

She had looked pretty with some makeup on and her hair combed back neatly. When she stood up from the bench near the hot dog stand, I realized she was much taller than Sarah. She wore a frilly demibra beneath her white blouse that exposed an ample wedge of breast flesh. Blushing like a teen, just coming from a landscaping job, I found myself giving her a tourist's thumbnail sketch of Northtown. She was vacationing on the Strip with a friend, she said. Her striking looks and flawless body were spoiled by one thing, however, and that was the pig she cavorted with, betrayed me with, and with whom she played me for a sucker.

"Marija," I said into the phone. "I thought you had gone back home."

"I got an extension of my visa. I've been in Cleveland every day over this, for one thing or another, but they finally gave me permission to stay another six months."

"Congratulations," I said.

"You sound strange."

"I'm... I'm peachy," I said.

"What is that, peachy?" She asked in a little-girl's whispery voice she probably learned from American soap operas.

"I don't think I could explain to you what's happened since... since that day," I said.

"Then explain it to me over a drink. I'll be in Rita's in twenty-five minutes."

She hung up on me. Phones don't have toggle buttons nowadays, but I could have hit one with my erection. Unlike my wife, I had not committed adultery. But in my mind I had cheated on her with this strange, exotic, and dangerous woman who had suddenly appeared in my life.

Here was my problem of the moment: I had no wheels and five bags of money at the bottom of a dirty swimming pool forty miles away. Jefferson-on-the-Lake might as well be on the moon. If I had known Sarah's boyfriend's number at that moment, I might have been desperate enough to ask to borrow our car.

Instead I called up my former boss's number and got his son-in-law.

"Rickie," I said.

"Who is this?"

"It's Jack," I said.

"What do you want, Trichaud?" He didn't sound pleased to be hearing from me.

"Rick, do you recall that landscaping job on Tanglewood three weeks back – the Japanese honeysuckle?"

"What of it?" His voice deepened a notch and revealed his antennae were on full alert.

"I need a favor, Rick."

"Shit, what kind of favor?"

"I need to borrow one of the trucks for a small errand. Shouldn't take me more than a couple hours," I said.

"No fucking way, Trichaud. I'm not letting you have-"

"Now, Rick, Rickie, lad. Is Tinker home? Put her on, please. Maybe your wife might be interested in hearing the more salient details of that particular landscaping job. Especially the part about where I'm outside baking in the sun for four hours while you, Rickster, old trout, you were inside riding the customer."

"Fuck you, you can't prove it," he said.

"I don't have to prove it, dummy. You'll have to prove your innocence to Tinker and her father. You know how many times I've heard Augie say he'd break the neck of any man-"

"What do you want?"

"I just told you, asshole. I need to borrow a ride for a couple hours. I'll have it right back. Tell Augie it's going on a job somewhere."

"I'll leave the key in it. Take the Ford. And, fuck me, if you put one scratch-"

Any conversation after that was a waste of my breath. Just as the old man had insisted all those years ago in my and Carlos' youth in the old section of Montreal: everybody's got a weakness. I thought of Marija's phone call and hated the fact he was always right.

#4

I took a cab over to Augie's and got off a block from the house. Rick had even parked the F-150 in the street for me. I was one of the few unemployed in the middle of the day. I'd lost track of the number of lines I was stepping across.

The daytime crowds on the Strip were dwindling down. There were no teenagers hanging out at the arcades on Little Minnesota. I hit the power button and turned it to channel three. I heard a crackle. I said one word and shut it off.

Rita's was dark and almost empty; the air inside had a heavy, fuggy smell of fermented beer that a kitchen match could ignite. She was sitting in a booth close to the bar.

The bartender was a different guy from the owner. He was about thirty-five and wore a trimmed van Dyke. His arms were muscular but bare of tattoos. A couple sat at a booth far from the bar and a solitary drinker sat hunched on his stool at the end of the bar concentrating hard on his beer can.

"Sit down, Jack."

"Where's Calderone?"

Marija thought about it for a while and discarded the lie she was formulating. It was a small enough compliment to my intelligence, I suppose.

"Randall's not far from here," she said. I hated the fact she called him by his Christian name, this oversized, tattooed biker lout with his Aryan Brotherhood connections.

"How's my brother doing?"

"That depends on you, Jack, now doesn't it?"

It was hard to see her features well even though she was close to me. Her lipstick was a shade of red so deep it made her whole face glow. She was beautiful and she was poison from the first day we met.

"What do you want?"

She laughed and her teeth were exposed to the gum line. She was a beauty in bad lighting too. "Isn't it obvious?" she said.

"Was I a part of it from the beginning or did my brother suggest me to Randall?"

"Does any of that matter now?"

"I suppose not."

"Good. Then let's talk about what we need to talk about."

"OK," I said. "You called me, remember?"

She took a sip of her beer. I watched her throat muscles work. "European beer is so much better," she said. I said something banal about Canadian beer.

"Simple enough," she said brightly. "The money for your brother."

I nodded my head slowly. I expected it yet I was hoping there would be other things that could be brought in as leverage before that. Randall had to be champing at the bit.

"Does he know?"

"Not yet but he's getting more agitated. Randall's not going back to jail and he's not going to hang around this dump of a town forever. Not with all these cops running around."

That seemed an odd thing to say, what with me being a cop magnet at the moment, but I let it go.

"We need to deal," she said, trying to sound tough. "Or he's gone and your brother will be found in some dumpster. He'll be in pieces."

"So for the time being, my brother's ignorant, is that what you're saying? He's just walking around with the Sword of Damocles over his head wherever you three are camping out."

"What sword?"

"It's, it's… Never mind. What else are we talking about?"

"What do you mean?"

Her features were close enough so that I could watch her mouth twist up into a look of annoyance.

"My brother and I came out of the same womb," I said after a pause. "That's all we have in common. If you think

I'm going to hand you nine hundred thousand dollars for sentimental reasons, you can tell Randall to kiss my ass with his tongue out."

"Do you know what he'll do to him?"

"If he's smarter than he looks, he'll cut his losses and run. He'll get as far away from my brother as he can get. I'd offer you the same advice if I thought you'd take it."

"That's not going to happen, Jack. You'll get pieces of your brother in the mail before that happens."

"I'm leaving now, Marija."

The anger that looked about to boil over disappeared and she dropped her shoulders a little. Her face assumed its normal prettiness.

"You need to understand something. Randall Calderone has friends. He knows people. Some of them are in prison and some of them are free – walking around, sitting in a bar having a beer like me. He just has to make a phone call and your life will be... changed. You don't want to spend all your life looking over your shoulder."

"I can handle it," I said. "Having money makes it easy."

"Look, we'll let you keep some of the money. That's only fair. You were in for a third, you can have a third."

"What if I want more?"

"We can negotiate," she said. "I can go under the table and suck you off right now. Would you like me to do that, Jack?"

I won't say I wasn't tempted, but I didn't say anything.

"Besides," she said, "I don't believe what you said about your brother."

"Why is that?"

"He never stops talking about the two of you. You're all

he thinks about. You and him, starting over. He's driving Randall crazy."

"That's a pretty short drive."

"You make stupid jokes but you won't find anything funny for much longer."

"I don't find anything funny now, Marija. I was living a normal, happy life a week ago before your thug boyfriend decided I needed to spice it up with a felony bank robbery and kidnapping that will guarantee I never see a sunset before they wheel me out at ninety-three."

"You can walk away from this with plenty of money and you can have your brother and your nice house all to yourselves and raise chickens."

"My house isn't so nice anymore," I said.

"We thought you needed a little push," she said.

"So all that fornication on the couch in my basement was purely for my benefit?"

"Jack," she said, and leaned across the bar toward me; her breasts expanded into the table's edge but didn't flatten much. I caught her smiling at me. She opened her denim jacket so I could read her tee-shirt: My Eyes Are Up Here. She would be the kind of girl to ask a guy how to shoot pool while rubbing her backside into his crotch. One painted nail raked the back of my wrist hard enough to leave a white scratch line.

"You know," I said, "I'll sound like every older woman you've ever known who tried to warn you about men. If you're lucky, you'll come to some day in a hospital or an alley. Randall's not the marrying kind, Marija."

"Let me worry about me," she said. "Let's say I like the relationship the way it is at the moment. Do you like a little pain with sex, Jack?"

"I don't know what sex is anymore. I'm not sure if my leg goes here or her leg goes there. I need one of those how-to books for beginners."

"Mmm, I'd love to show you how to again. Why don't we go back to my cabin? You know where it is, right? You've been there before."

"I know where it is," I said.

"Shy boy, you're blushing! Did you like what you saw, hmmm?" Her hand reached under the table and caressed me.

"Shouldn't we be focusing on the split, Marija?"

"Yes, give me your hand. You can have that split right now. It's already wet."

I pulled my hand free.

"Want to lick it? I can feel how hard you are. Come on, let's go back to my cabin and fuck like rabbits."

Her hand roamed again seeking my crotch. I picked it off delicately like removing a foraging tarantula.

"OK," she said. "You had your chance. If I leave here, you'll never see your brother alive."

"I'll make the swap," I said. "But not here and not today."

"Where's the money?"

"Close by," I said. "It's close."

"Now's as good a time as any, Jack. Let's do this and go our separate ways. I don't think I can hold Randall off much longer," she said. "You don't know."

"That would be a bad idea," I said and leaned back against the frayed and dank-smelling naugahyde of the booth.

"Why is it a bad idea, Jack?" She could swing her moods like a metronome on a Steinway between a soft purl and a harsh alto.

"Because the bartender is an undercover agent. I've had two more following me since I left town. One's a big tall black FBI guy from Youngstown. He'd have followed me in here, but I guess he didn't want to stick out in his Armani suit."

Her eyes tightened and locked onto mine; the frown lines disfigured the beauty of that face. She whipped her head around. The bartender was talking to the solo drunk.

"How do you know that?"

"Ask my brother," I said. "We were taught surveillance by one of the best."

#5

I drove back with my escorts well behind me because there wasn't any traffic on Lake Road to hide behind. Instead of taking the road by the lake all the way to Walnut as usual, I hit the fork where it tees off a state route that leads through some undeveloped acreage and connects to the I90. The road is bad and narrow. The big Ford engine gave me all the power I needed to disappear down it. I hit the first gulley at eighty-two and left the road surface at the top of the hill.

The next gully was trickier because it veered slightly to right and came up fast. I slowed to 75 but even that wasn't enough to keep my wheels from going airborne. The right front tire struck gravel and I knew I was in trouble. I was patient and didn't ease off the gas pedal until I felt the back and front tires hold their own against the spin-out. Little by little, I wrestled it back and reclaimed the road. It was a straight shot to the first caution light on West 19th and then a short, sharp turn down Cemetery. I'd had a driver's license in Michigan forfeited when I first discovered the joy of speeding.

I stopped before Cemetery ran out where four houses were all crammed together into opposite sides of the street. I reversed it into a vacant lot overgrown with crab grass and rabbitfoot clover near a transformer unit enclosed by a small cyclone fence.

They were better than I thought. The first Crown Victoria went sailing past just five minutes later. Pippin wasn't either of the two drivers I glimpsed.

I waited another fifteen and then he came by at a slow thirty m.p.h. He didn't want to chance getting stuck in the small ditch that separated the road from the field so he exited the car and walked. He picked his way through the scrub where I had most of the truck secreted and worked his way gingerly to my window. From his knees to his cuffs he was covered with cockleburs and dandelion seeds. He hadn't taken more than a couple steps before he sneezed.

"Ragweed pollen," he said. "My allergies are going crazy right now."

"It's the season for it," I said.

"So, tell me why you're sitting in a patch of weeds, Jack?"

"They're not all weeds. Look around you, Pippin. I see Fire Pink and Indian Blanket. You're stepping on Musk

Mallow with your right foot, and just behind you is a Sweet Pepperbrush."

"Do you want to know what I see? I see a landscaper playing a very, very stupid game." Pippin put both be-ringed and manicured hands across my window; he was almost tall enough to look me right in the eye.

"Is that what we're doing?"

"Not me, Jack. You and me, we're not playing a game. You're my job." He didn't raise his voice or show me any annoyance. "So what do you think you're doing out here in the middle of nowhere?"

"I was thinking of tacos," I said.

"Tacos," he repeated. He nodded as if that made perfect sense.

"I know a good Mexican restaurant in town. Not far from here," I said.

"I'll follow you," he said. "That million dollars burning a hole in your pocket?"

"You see that green flower near the fence there?" I pointed to a spot near my outside tire. "It's Wild Sarsaparilla. You should take some with you and boil it up. It'll help your allergies."

"Thanks, Grandma Moses, but I'll stick with modern medicine."

#6

He must have contacted the other agents while I was in the bathroom washing my hands because I saw his cell phone had been relocated to the other side of his sports jacket. The staff at Three Amigos were all young Mexican men and women. Most were bilingual.

"What's good?"

"Sarah – she's my wife or my ex-wife, I should say – and I have tried everything on the menu. I like the Santa Fe quesadilla with shrimp and steak strips. Watch out for the green chilies, but everything else is mild."

"I don't care for Mex food," Pippin said scowling at the menu. "Everything looks like the taco in disguise. Besides, my appetite's off today."

I set the menu aside and dipped a corn chip shaped like hibiscus petals into the salsa.

"Sometimes they have a mariachi band," I said. "You're supposed to put the tip money in the hole in the guitar after they play a set at your table. I didn't realize that the first time and I embarrassed Sarah. I didn't know that."

"You don't get around much, do you?"

"Not as much as I used to," I said.

"What does tipping a mariachi band have to do with anything, Jack? What do these blue corn chips," he plucked one from the bowl and flipped it at me, "have to do with a stolen million dollars you and your knuckleheaded friends took?"

A young couple with two small children stopped eating and looked at us.

"Sorry," he said and smiled at them. The smile disappeared when he turned it at me. "Getting jerked around like this makes me very unhappy, Jack."

"Try some chips. It'll get the juices going again."

"I've spent the morning with a handkerchief soaked in that BCI agent's cheap cologne wrapped around my face because of the stench of a dead body's intestinal juices. A week of being stored in a garage rolled up in his own living room carpet doesn't do much for the decomp so, if you don't mind, let's just order and not talk about the cuisine."

After a moment or two of silence, I felt him looking hard at me, a cop's auger.

"Don't play dumb behind that menu, Trichaud. It doesn't suit you and it insults my intelligence. Your buddy Calderone's erstwhile employer, some cat named Jonas

Fullilov Gomes, late of Youngstown, former proprietor of a roofing business supplemented by a little fencing and a little narcotics trade and some other minor scams we don't need to go into, had a connection to Calderone. They both did time at Riker's."

"Sorry. I never heard of him," I said.

That much was true. But I had a memory of Calderone arguing with my brother about making a quick side trip to Youngstown the day after they showed up at my place – something about a 'loose end' to be tied off. Calderone never used a name, but I inferred it was somebody he had done time with before Dannemora and wasn't too happy with.

"Yeah, well, if any forensics comes back that says you did," Pippin growled around a corn chip, "there ain't gonna be any sweetheart deals with any federal judges I know."

"What do you mean?"

"Ten years," Pippin said. He picked something out of his teeth and made a show of looking at it with disgust. "Ten to life for complicity. Deal's off it turns out you did more than fetch and drive."

"Ten years," I said.

"Federal time means no good time, no parole. Fox-Whitcomb still won't ID you, so you don't have kidnapping charges tacked on. You can do the time in Lewisburg or Atlanta, where you won't bump into any Aryan Brother friends of Calderone on a daisy chain."

"Until I met Calderone, I wouldn't have known one to trip over."

"Well, you seem to blend in rather well considering your little adventures this past week. You mean you didn't have to do all that stiff-arming and shouting 'White Power!' 'Hail to Youth!' and all that Nazi crap?"

"My brother must have gotten involved after my visit to him. He had no tattoos and he never talked any of that Nazi twaddle when we were boys growing up," I said.

"Something he picked up between shop classes, huh? Look, Trichaud, you think I give a shit about that 'Fourteen-Words-Heil-Hitler' horseshit because I'm a black man?"

"What fourteen words?"

"Man, pull my other leg, the one with bells on it. I'm not buying any of your know-nothing act. I grew up in Cabrini Green, Chicago. We invented that don't-know-nothin'-about-nothin' shit in the ghetto."

"I don't know where my brother is. I think he's somewhere near Jefferson-on-the-Lake, maybe holed up in a cabin somewhere off the Strip," I said.

"Give us some credit. We've checked the registration of every cabin out there. We've checked every known Brand member, skinhead, neo-Nazi and bike gang member from here to Kalamazoo. Nobody's whispered anything in my shell-like ear so far. DEA keeps informants in every chapter of bike trash that ride through Jefferson-on-the-Lake – the Ching-a-lings, the Pagans, the Mongols, and Hell's Angels."

"Calderone's staying with a woman named Marija Ercegovic," I said.

"Keep farting around like this, Jack, and I'm going to let that BCI fellow take you in for some serious questioning. They told me you'll crack like a walnut inside of twenty minutes."

He looked at me again. The people in the booth next to us were listening.

"How's the Tejada Tampico?" he asked.

"Salty but not too spicy," I said. "Your stomach can handle it."

The outside air had a real chill to it. The sun went down faster each day now and stayed farther west. "Thanks," I said to Pippin, who was groaning and holding his stomach.

"De nada," he said. "They tenderized the living hell out that steak." I watched as Pippin folded some bills into his wallet.

"I tried to tell you."

The stars were already beginning to etch themselves against the parts of the sky shifting from violet to cobalt.

"I'll be seeing you soon, Trichaud."

"Not if I see you first, Special Agent Pippin."

I parked the truck out front of Augie's where I had picked it up. Augie's house was brightly lit and I saw shadows moving back and forth across the drawn blinds and shades. I had worked for him for nine years but I didn't have any feelings one way or the other about it. The nearest pay phone was down on Bridge Street, so I decided to walk back instead of call a cab.

I wanted to go home and crash on the floor. Sleep my blank and mindless dreams. Awake in a new world, some other universe besides the one I was born into. I would have bartered my existence for the short life of a sewer rodent.

The walk did me some good. I even worked up a sweat. The back of my neck and chest were damp with perspiration.

I passed the lights of shops closed for the day. Some sold provender to the recreational boats but most were second-hand goods stores that used words like 'antiques' and 'boutique' in the windows. I passed by a couple of the seedier bars where the locals all knew one another and turned into the Suomi Café, the harbor's closet thing to a fern bar. It mixed a lot of demographics in its clientele. Rumor was that crack and meth were sold out of the bar with the owner's blessing. Around ten o'clock the casual drinkers and the middle-aged crowd disappeared; the signal was usually the appearance of the first black male who came in.

I took a seat at the bar. A blonde college-aged girl served me a bottle of Pabst, and I drank a few sips of it. I made it last for an hour and then I ordered another one. The bar was mostly young people now, loud and gregarious. I might as well have had a Plexiglass cone dropped over me. The seats around me were occupied by several men and two girls, who all found someone or a group to party with. I ordered my third drink and was in the act of polishing it off, eager to call it a night.

In the mirror back home I saw my haggard face and was shocked by what I saw. I looked ten years older. They say everybody in the world has a fox face or a pig face. The thickness of my face was gone, all the softness of the Sarah years, and I saw a different face staring back at me.

"I'm not like you," I said to the mirror. "I'm not you."

The mirror didn't say anything back. They also say mirrors don't lie.

WEDNESDAY, SEPTEMBER 8

10:11 A.M.

#7

I was greeted by two city policemen who showed me a search warrant for the house and grounds. They asked me if I would be willing to go down to the station for an interview, and I said I might if I knew what this concerned. They said it was regarding the recent activities of Carlos Maurice Trichaud.

Outside on the porch a team of forensics people with their gear stood around in the yard drinking coffee. The cop leading me said to them, "Try not to mess anything up in there," which made the other cop snicker. When he put me in the back seat of the cruiser, he said, "I'll bet your neighbors just love what you do for property values."

At the station they escorted me to a different room, and asked me if I wanted to waive my rights to having a lawyer present. I asked if this was about my brother or me, and Pippin shrugged.

"I'll waive my rights," I said.

The detective said, "The officer who picked you up said you wanted to make a phone call before you left the house. Were you going to call a lawyer?"

"No, I just wanted to know if my phone was tapped."

"How would you know that from a phone call, Jack?"

"I wouldn't," I said.

Pippin smiled, the lawyer lurking within the cop guessed it. "Fruit of the poison tree, right? You think you can get any evidence we collect thrown out of court if this comes to trial and the phone trap was unwarranted."

"You think like a criminal, Trichaud," the officer said. "That doesn't make you look innocent to us."

"Who among us is innocent?"

"OK, Jesus of Northtown," Pippin said. "Let's cut the shit."

#8

What followed was a two-hour, intensive grilling that skirted direct questions of my involvement. Pippin and the detective double-teamed me hard. Forget good cop-bad cop; they hammered me with questions and wouldn't let me think or finish a sentence. They'd have hours to go over the tape scrutinizing my responses, but I had fractions of a second to think and worry about the lies twisting around my feet and dragging me down. Now I was on record as having said certain things that, if later contradicted by facts, would nail me along with Calderone and my brother.

Pippin walked me out of the building. He offered me a ride but I declined.

"Come on, don't be stubborn, Jack. You knew this was coming. You should be grateful you're allowed to walk out of there."

"What weren't you telling me back there?"

"Let's walk. My car's in the back," he said.

I got in and he turned off the radio as soon as the car started. It was set to the same classical station in Youngstown that Sarah listened to when we went for long drives in the country.

"Sorry about that," he said.

"I think Pehrlman's a little rough with that one Brahms sonata," I said.

Pippin's face widened into a grin. His skin almost matched the mahogany leather of the seats.

"Gee whiz, I don't know what to make out of you, Jack. I really don't. I did a deep background on you and got nothing." He laughed and put the car into drive. "I don't even know if you should be in this country, man. You and your brother have birth certificates in Minneapolis and then you disappear for fourteen years. Your brother turns up branded with swastikas spouting that ZOG nonsense in Dannemora..."

He looked at me hard. "That your thing, Jack? 'Holocaust Two – coming to a town near you.' That you?"

"I'm just an equal-opportunity hater," I said.

Pippin resumed his recitation of my biography, driving through caution lights and barely slowing down for stops – a man who took chances with life in small ways would take chances in big ways.

"You disappear off the radar until you turn up in this burgh nine years ago and you become a model citizen. You get a job, you pay your taxes, get married. You even go to church, for God's sake," Pippin snickered.

"Is that supposed to be a joke, Forzell?"

"Your zany life is a joke. Who are you? Your brother's IQ should have put him in Mensa. Instead he's telling the prison shrink he had to shave his head because a generation of panty hoses for women and electric hair dryers for men have shamed him into becoming a skinhead. You're a minimum-wage laborer working for his boss' son-in-law, who by the way nearly shit himself when we asked questions about you. He acted as if he barely remembered you."

"Things happen, Pippin. Did you plan your life so that everything went your way?"

"Gee, no, but unlike you, I pretty much stayed the course. Bachelor's degree CUNY, Columbia Law, Quantico, and except for a teensy misstep that landed me in Youngstown, I followed my game plan. I didn't take time out to rob the Bank of New York. I didn't wake up one morning and start trying my damnedest to make it onto America's Most Wanted. "

"I told you everything about me back there," I said.

"Yeah, yeah. And except for the facts we know, which are the only ones we can corroborate, nothing quite substantiates."

"Maybe you and these town cops should have got off your backsides, forgotten about me, and started a grid search around Jefferson-on-the-Lake."

"What makes you so sure he's there?"

"I'm not. I don't know," I said.

"That woman you met back in the biker's bar. She the

reason for your divorce and all this midlife crisis?"

"You're following her and you have my phone tapped so you might tell me what she has to do with it," I said.

"Yeah, we're on her and we've got leads. This isn't going to go away like that smell in your garage that's driving the sheriff's cadaver dog nuts."

"You indict on smells now?'"

Pippin laughed. "Come on, Jack. The first thing they teach us is to control the interview. You don't get to ask the questions, my boy. Let me help you. Give me something to work with." His face looked sincere but I've been acting without a script most of my life.

"How do I know this isn't about the money?"

"Your brother will have to take his chances, but everybody at the DA is in line with the federal proposal. Ten years, one-time offer. It goes away as soon as things change."

"Things like, say, Alicia Fox-Whitcomb changing her mind?"

"That, certainly, and whether your two co-conspirators decide to kill anyone in the line of duty while fleeing a felony arrest. Next stop, death row, Lucasville. Too bad they stopped using the chair in this state." He made a wry face. "Hell, a man's eyeballs'd explode out of his head. The body would stay hot on the slab for days afterward. Now the best we can hope for is somebody getting the lethal dosage wrong. Not much fun in that. "

"What if I do tell you where the money is?"

"That would be a good start."

"I'll call you," I said.

He leaned toward me and said, "Why is it I have the

feeling you timed this whole conversation just so you could say that as I pulled up to the curb?"

I shut the door and walked up the sidewalk to my house. It looked haggard and toothless like an old man's face.

The search teams might have been inspired by the mess they found. I found broken dishware on the kitchen floors and some bird photos tossed into a corner. Someone had slit the backings. I pulled the attic ladder down and climbed up. Dozens of feet had trampled through the soot that came wafting through the vents and cracks. A dozen plastic totes were emptied on the floor and every keepsake of Sarah's she didn't want me to throw out was unwrapped and tossed aside like so much junk. I suppose that's all it was, finally.

In a small room off the main floor of the attic I kept an old print of an L. Ron Hubbard sci-fi scene: a woman in a clingy spacesuit with a lot of cleavage showing was standing next to a spaceship on an alien planet with three suns. Sarah won it in a contest at the bookstore in the mall. I hated to sacrifice the frame, but it was one of my first fix-it jobs when we moved in. I had nailed the painting against a gaping hole where the north wind came whistling through the missing clay shingles and the holes in the rafters. Behind the painting, right between the studs, dangled the walkie-talkie from a ten-pound fishing line.

I took it downstairs and set it on the kitchen window shelf between a potted plant and an avocado seed suspended in a glass of water by toothpicks. Somehow they had survived all the commotion. I didn't think Randall Calderone would send a second contact out in the open like

Marija so soon, especially with the surveillance I was drawing, but second-guessing him was proving harder than I expected.

I took a big knife with me into the living room and cleared a place to sit in the corner with my back against the wall. I had a clear view through the open door, and both corner windows and the big picture window were minus curtains or shades so I would see anyone out there. I had booby-trapped the back door with fishing line and wind chimes. No Semtec but it would make a loud ruckus if anyone tried to come at me that way.

I pushed the junk aside and watched the insects crawling among the wrappers. The smell in the living room was acquiring strength from the onions in the discarded sandwich wrappers. Silverfish, centipedes and flies were drawn. Whenever a bug crawled too close, I tried to nail him with my butcher knife, and except for ladybugs which bring good luck, I stabbed everything within reach. I was choosing like God.

A saffron-yellow band of light came closer as time passed. I counted how many minutes it took to reach the tip of my foot and then my ankle and then my calf. By the time it reached my belt buckle, I was on the verge of sleep. The drone of the flies woke me up. I realized it was the zsss-zsss of the walkie-talkie. "That you, fuckface? That you, fucking asshole? Come in."

I fetched it from the kitchen shelf and thumbed the send button. "Fuckface stepped out for a minute, Randall. Can I take a message?"

"Your brother wants to speak to you."

"Jack, Jack? Come in, Jack?"

"Go ahead, Carlos."

"Hey, you alone?"

"No cops around if that's what you mean."

"What's that noise?"

"I've got the water running," I said.

"Ha, following the old man, ain't you, bro? Man, we have so much catching up to do. So many crazy times to talk about."

"These are the crazy times, Carlos. Can you talk?"

"My main man here is watching my back. I thought I could count on my own brother for that, too. I guess I got fucked again, eh?"

He sounded high, and I wondered how much I could say that he would understand. We were good at this as kids with adults around, but that was a long time ago and a lot of water had flowed over that dam.

"How close are you?" I asked.

"Very close but, ah, you got company like from one end of the street to the other, so it's not easy. The cops put snipers on the second floor of that house across the street. Imagine they're watching you right now."

"No one can see me from the back of the house," I said. My survey out the window showed me flocks of gulls fluttering and settling like white dusting on the peaks of the coal piles and a Great Lakes Company tug leading a ship to dock. The big crane siren warbled to bring in the dockworkers. White caps rolled all the way to the horizon and waves bursting ashore broke high over the breakwall to spill their foam over the giant rocks. Way down there Monarch butterflies were beginning to assemble for their long migration south.

"I didn't see the Jeep go by," I said.

"Shit almighty, man, that Jeep's too hot. Thanks to you, we had to ditch it-"

I heard Randall's angry voice behind him. My brother said: "I ain't telling him shit, man. Lighten up, eh?"

"So what do you want, Carlos?"

"What do I want?" He laughed. "I want the money, Jack! I... We want the money. The money, the money! The money that is mine. We want the money, you fucking-"

I heard a loud crash like a bag of rice hitting floorboards. Randall's voice came over: "You been talking to the cops, motherfucker?"

"Of course, I have, you moron. They've interviewed me twice. This morning for two hours. They want me to give them the money and they want me to testify against you and Carl."

"You're trying to piss me off, Jack, ain't you? It ain't gonna work. I know you ain't giving us up because Marija said you woulda done it by now. Let's say we got us a Mexican stalemate."

"A Mexican stalemate is when it's an even match, dummy. I've got all the money. You've got cops hunting for you. They're out there going twenty-four seven – hundreds of them from every police force and federal agency between here and the North Pole. They're going to squeeze you into a small corner, Randall."

"That baggage you spoke of, jackoff. One of it's got your brother's name on it. I will send it to you a piece at a time. You know I will do that."

"Don't try to engage me in debate, Randall. Stick to what you know best."

"You motherfucking cocksucking son of a diseased whore-"

"There you go."

"You heard me, bitch! We want the money. It's mine! I'm sending her for it. You better have it ready or say goodbye to your brother because I'll cut his fucking head off and stick it on a pole on my way out of town!"

"There are people watching me every second," I said. "I can't move."

"I'll gut this dope fiend on the floor like a fish in twenty-four hours. You fucking figure out how to get the money to her, smart boy, but you get it right because you got you exactly one chance."

"Tell me where to meet her," I said.

"She'll call you. Keep the walkie-talkie on you, no fuckin' cell phones."

"Let me speak to my brother."

"Eat shit, motherfucker!"

#9

My phone rang an hour later. I retreated back to my sunlit corner. I was in the last rounds and losing by a wide margin. No knockdowns yet, but I had nobody to help me find a way to beat my opponent.

The phone rang. I let the machine catch it.

My father was always big on phone numbers. He used to test us by asking us to commit five different phone numbers plus area codes and foreign exchange numbers to memory. He'd leave us alone in a dark closet, and then he'd come back in fifteen minutes. He told us to repeat the numbers while screaming in our faces. You couldn't leave the closet until you had all the numbers committed to memory. I spent a lot of sleepless nights in that closet until fatigue and slaps replaced the old man's barking in my ear. Carlos rarely missed. He had a photographic memory. I'd come staggering out at dawn, bleary-eyed and brain-fatigued, and almost fall asleep at the breakfast table while he'd eat his cereal and mock me for being a thick-headed imbecile. My father would be sitting right there across from him lurking behind the newspapers as if all was normal in a normal household.

I called Marija's phone outside her cabin.

She picked up on the eighth ring. "Hello."

"Don't say anything," I said. "Remember where you sat in the booth?"

"Yes, shall I meet you at the same time?"

"An hour later, and take the next booth over, if you don't mind. I still have splinters from the oak benches in that room."

Crude but she'd understand. I needed a few minutes alone with her before they could set up.

#10

It was time to arrange transportation. I dialed Rick's number and got Tinker.

"Hello, Jack, did you want Rick?"

"Yes, Tink, I hope it's no trouble."

"I never got to say I was sorry, Jack, about the job and everything," she said.

'Everything,' I supposed, was Sarah. Although the four of us met at their place for barbecue and drinks a few times socially, we weren't close. Rick's obnoxious personality dictated that. I liked Tinker but she had more mood swings than a cat. She was also badly spoiled by Augie and reckless when she was drunk. Sarah was shooting pool in the house with Rick one night early this summer; she and I sat on the patio sipping Sea Breezes when she raised up her top. Her breasts were cup-sized with wrinkled areolas and nipples. Before she married Rick, she broke up a marriage in some wife-swapping scenario according to Sarah's gossip.

"No need to apologize at all," I said. "I was hoping Rick would be able to give me a reference for a job I have lined up."

"That's wonderful, Jack. I'm sure he'd be glad to. Here he is," she said and handed the phone to him. There was a long hiatus while husband and wife stuff went on and finally I heard Rick's exasperated snarl: "Christ, what do you want from me now, Trichaud?"

"Rick, I need to borrow the truck tonight."

"You want to bor- Do you have any idea... do you know some fucking FBI agent was asking-"

"Rickie, before you blow out a blood vessel in your tiny brain, listen to me. This isn't a request. If that truck isn't out in front of your house by the time I get there, I'm coming in for an intense conversation with Tinker. You will be shitting blood for a week because her old man will start pounding on your kidneys."

"You're not fucking human, Trichaud. You're not human. What kind of man does that to a friend? I broke bread with you in my house."

"Twenty minutes," I said.

I called a cabbie and got a different driver. She was a chunky woman in a butch haircut and wore her sleeves rolled so high up her thick arms I saw the bottom half of a valentine tattoo with an arrow through the center. It read

Cinda-Lin Forever, but it had been crudely done in a wavering black script and was faded.

I gave her the address and she asked me a few questions about some streets in that area.

"Don't get too many calls to that side of town," she said.

"How's Cinda-Lin?" I said.

"Who?"

I pointed at the tattoo.

"Shee-it, man, I dumped that bitch ten years ago. She was my first old lady when I got out of Marysville."

She told how she lured her ex-husband out of a bar with a story about his ailing mother and then gut-shot him with an over-and-under.

"Was he abusive?"

"Hell no," she laughed. "I used to whip up on him every day. Man was a goddamn pussy but he had this wang was about a yard long."

"So why did you leave him?"

She turned around and showed me a set of stained dentures. "That was it, see? A mile of dick but no balls."

She found it hilarious that the then-governor let a whole bunch of women out when he left office – all for killing spouses. "We was abused, see?" She laughed again, cheered by the memory of life's amazing turnabouts.

When she dropped me off, I overtipped her by twenty dollars. "Like, who you want me to kill, man?" she said. But when she saw my face, the laugh died.

"I'm tempted but no thanks," I said. "My name is Jack. Nice to meet you, and thanks for the ride. Maybe I'll ask for you next time."

She said, "You got any more like you where you're at,

buddy?"

My old man used to say that cab drivers were priceless sources of information and useful contacts. Don't be a snob, he said to us. Use the little people around you the way you use objects close at hand in a street fight. His favorite example was to drive your opponent's back into a streetlamp if it had a sharp end so you could blow his back out or, with luck, sever his spinal cord. He read the classics (I never believed him) but he liked to quote a favorite Roman maxim: *Homo hominis lupus est*. 'Man is a wolf to man.'

#11

I took the truck and drove the speed limit to Jefferson-on-the-Lake. Once or twice, I thought I saw headlights loom up behind me and then drop back. Traffic was heavy once I turned the last curve and followed the flow into the main strip. This was the last big holiday of the summer, the weekend the heist was supposed to have gone down.

Ten thousand people would come through this street in the next thirty-six hours; most would walk the street or sit and people-watch, eat cotton candy and pizza or sidewalk shish kebab; a few would drink too much in the bars and get into scraps. A lot of sex would happen in a short time without a lot of romantic prelude. Some of it would be illicit, some of it your garden-variety infidelities. I headed for the place where most of the illegal sex would commence.

Fleas bite harder in September when they sense the beginning of cold weather. It's the same thing with hookers at Jefferson-on-the-Lake. The older ones, especially the ones with meth addiction, get more aggressive in pursuit of the dollar, and it's all the tiny, ill-trained police force can do to keep fellatio from being performed on drunks in plain view of the out-of-towners strolling the side streets with their children. Labor Day signals the end of the season, the last chance for a good time.

I knew it would be crowded and I was right. I hadn't been down Little Minnesota since last summer when Sarah and I drove through.

Maybe Marija put me in mind of it, but I had forgotten until now. She was a teenager, probably a runaway, standing alone on the corner and unusual only because she had that white-blonde hair of translucent blondes; her Lycra miniskirt went up to her buttocks. Sarah asked me if I'd like to have her, and I laughed. "That wasn't a test question," she told me. I recalled the look on her face: she was serious. "Both of us," she said. "Tonight." I let the moment pass and soon she was gone in the rearview mirror. When Sarah was riding me that night, she looked into my eyes but I knew she was thinking about that girl.

#12

I drove back to Northtown and stopped at a plaza where I ate at a Chinese restaurant. The young woman who ran it saw me come in and spoke some Chinese to her husband at the stove; she didn't wait for my order. I never ordered anything else. Just across from the Main Moon past a weed-strewn lot was another small plaza almost entirely deserted except for a new business agency which had a lurid green-and-yellow neon sign advertising the words Cash Advance. Things were so bad in Northtown even the topless bar had gone out of business. While my dinner was being prepared, I walked over to the pay phone and called the cabbie's number. I left a message for her with the dispatcher and said where I would be.

I was cracking open my fortune cookie when she walked in. It said that I was 'well-liked' and had 'many friends.'

"You called me for a cab," she said.

"Have a fortune cookie," I said. "Would you like something to eat?"

"Naw, I'm on the clock, man. So you need a ride or what?"

"I'll pay for your time," I said and lifted my left hand to show her the three twenties curled beneath it.

"In that case I wouldn't mind a bowl of that chicken soup and some of that there egg foo yung you're eating."

"It's egg drop soup and shrimp lo mein."

"Egg drop, whatever," she said. "All the same to me, man."

"Have a seat," I said.

"I'll radio my dispatcher, say I'm on lunch break."

She must have carried over the convict's habit of eating close to the plate. Calderone ate like that, a dog with its face into the bowl. I drank some green tea and waited for her.

"Man alive, that was fuckin' tasty," she said. "I'd love me a fuckin' cigarette right now."

"I'll pay and meet you in the cab," I said.

The cab reeked of smoke but it was doubtful anybody would think of complaining to the company behind her back. Stevie – that was her name – carried an aura of good-natured menace.

"Here's a fifty for your trouble, Stevie. Tell your dispatcher whatever you want about the fare."

"Don't worry, I will," she said and tucked the bill into her shirt pocket. "But you didn't call me over here because you just had a sudden urge to buy me Chinese, did you?"

"I've got a proposal for you," I said. "It might sound a little bizarre and I won't answer any questions about it. You just need to know I'll pay well. If you decline, there's a hundred for your trouble. If you want the job, it's worth a thousand more to me."

"Jesus wheezus, lay it on me, dude," she said. "For that much, I'll go down on a dead cop."

I told her what I wanted done, and she looked at me with a squint. She asked me a lot of questions, but they were the right kinds of questions.

"I can manage the one part easy enough," she said and nodded her head slowly, thinking about it. "Fuckin' town's got 'em all over the fuckin' place. Nobody'll miss one. Getting it there at the time you want it? Well, shit, that's the problem," she said. "But you say you can't tell me where?"

"Not yet but soon."

"You ain't giving me much to work with."

"One thousand dollars," I said.

"Look, I'm gonna need me a partner and a flatbed or something," she said. "Cost you another five for the welder."

That would take the last of my reserve cash down to four hundred and some change. It was cutting it close, but my options were limited.

"Five," I said. "Half now." I counted out the money and gave it to her to count.

"Here's a number if you have to call me. Ring twice,

hang up and call again. Two rings. I'll dial you right back at your company number, but I don't know how long that number's going to be good."

"No, use my cell," she said and scribbled a number for me. She handed it to me and I handed it right back.

"What's the matter?"

"I have it," I said.

"You're one strange mo'fucker, Jack," she said with that squint heavy smokers develop.

"I've been told that a lot lately," I said.

#13

I wasn't surprised to see Agent Pippin sitting on my porch when I got back to the house. "Door's open, Agent Pippin," I said. "Come on in."

"You might want to do something about that before winter," he said.

"You know how it is when you're pressed for time," I said.

"Yes, as a matter of fact, I do. There's a big building on the corner of Ninth and Pennsylvania in DC that's using up all my minutes and wearing out my telex. They want to know why two brainless lowlifes are still running around Northeast Ohio with close to a million dollars."

"So how is it going, Agent Pippin – your progress, I mean?"

"Getting there, Jack, getting there. It is coming together fine and I thank you for asking."

"I don't suppose you'd be willing to confide any bureau secrets about the whereabouts of Randall Calderone?"

"Right again, Jack."

"Do you mind if I make some coffee?"

"How many cups do you drink, my friend?"

"The number varies. It depends on the particular crisis of the day," I said.

"Then I'd say you're consuming gallons of it lately."

"You didn't drive up from Youngstown to enquire about my caffeine intake."

"Actually I don't spend much time down there nowadays. I've got a motel off the freeway. Comfy but the porn's unsatisfying. Like you, Jack. A lot of prick-teasing without the Big O."

"Sorry you're feeling so unsatisfied, Agent Pippin. Maybe you should drive home more often for a conjugal visit. Or try more coffee."

"You're mixing metaphors now, aren't you, Jack?"

"Maybe but I'm confused about what we're really talking about," I said.

"Confused is something I know about. Here's one thing you might clear up for me. Your father, for starters. I got stonewalled when I sent your father's name over to Langley, see if maybe your family was on some kind of post-Nine Eleven list. My guy over there did some private checking. All he could reveal was your father was GS-13. That's two pay grades higher than mine. You never once mentioned that fact with all that talking you did downtown. How come?"

"It wasn't germane," I said.

He laughed. "Ger-mane. Now, that's a big word for a guy who never went past grammar school. Interpol has nothing on you, but the RCMP telexed me a couple tidbits. You were an active youngster, weren't you?"

I knew he was fishing. The Canadian courts wouldn't release any facts of my incarceration as a young-adult offender, but he'd know I was a ward of Ontario for a while. I had done a couple months in a Toronto city jail when I left Quebec and was learning how to live on the streets. Even Sarah didn't know about that.

"Man, the things you didn't say. You living in Montreal, and you never mentioned that one, either. All that bullshit about going to a tiny parochial school in Minneapolis in the cold, dark winters – oh my. You jes' pullin' my dick, wasn't you, white boy?"

"Is that your way of keeping it real, Agent Pippin? You wear those fine-looking suits that say you're proud to be a successful professional, but how many Afro-Americans are there in the bureau? All window dressing for the quota system, isn't it?"

"I notice you keep trying to put a burr under my saddle, Jack. That comment about my field darkie shuck and jive – keeping it real. Old slang, man. Better get on Facebook or some shit. Find out how the kids are talking these days."

"I'll consider that suggestion. Thanks."

"You think I'm some affirmative-action baby you can mess with. This is the fucking US government talking to you."

"It's hard to read you, Forzell," I said.

"I can see you're fishing now. I can see that," he said. "You want me to tell you things, but that ain't how it works, Jack."

He wagged a finger at me playfully. He kept the smile fastened but it was a little tighter at the corners than before.

"Why not put Calderone on your Ten Most Wanted list – do something useful instead of wasting time on me?"

"You watch too much TV, man. Two reasons, but first let me answer your question. Calderone is small potatoes. Your brother, he don't even count. You need to kill a couple state troopers or hang out with serious terrorists you want on that list, my boy. I did submit his name, for what it's worth, but the DDA didn't send it on."

"You said two reasons."

"You're making a lot of moves, Jack. Borrowing trucks, cruising the Strip. I got reports on you from all over. Were you looking for some of that young snatch now that your wife has dumped you? Is that it? Get a little sport-fucking in before the metal doors clang shut behind you for the rest of your natural life?"

"Something like that," I said.

"Here's some advice for your near future. Put all thoughts of that out of your head because where you're going, they make cute little punks like you wear dresses and they change their names to Mary. You're too old and ugly for that, maybe, but you better learn to sleep with one eye open, keep a sharpened bed coil handy, and get used to dating the Palm sisters."

"Thanks, I'll bear it in mind. But it's still not worth your time to drive over from your comfy motel room," I said.

"Third reason, then. I got a line on Calderone from the DEA while he was in the Southwest. They say he worked for the Ciudad Juárez cartel moving drugs out of Neuvo Laredo across the Texas border. They use Uzis down there, Jack. They drip acid on their victims. They soak rags in kerosene and tie them around the victims' balls before they light them on fire. They burn snitches alive in fifty-gallon barrels."

"Again, I say, why tell me?"

"Your brother's chum, Calderone, he fits right in. One of my DEA sources said a gringo matching his description working for the Jiminez brothers walked into a bar called La Portena and set five decapitated heads on top of the bar, walked out whistling Dixie."

My guts were still churning from the revelation that my father might actually have been a legitimate intelligence agent. All those stories, all that James Bond wacko stuff like being a top-level intelligence agent in Cambodia during Pol Pot's regime. Carlos never quite let go of the illusions we used to have about him. From fifteen on, I never believed that everything he said was anything but another scrap of twisted fantasy from a deranged man who failed at life...

Pippin's voice took me back to the present. "He didn't just cut their heads off," he was saying, "but, man, he skinned their faces, one at a time – took the flesh right off the bones with a filleting knife. Five of them! A lot of those Brand assholes are tough and maybe could do one if you were strong enough to stomach it. But five, no way."

It gave me a chill to think I had anything in common

with Randall Calderone. I made a show of checking my watch.

"Oh, sorry. Am I boring you?" Pippin asked with mock-seriousness. "Well, let me cut to the chase, as they say. Alicia Fox-Whitcomb is making another statement today. I do believe she's finally going to recant and name your ass. You like big words, don't you? She's finally going to make that third identification, Jack."

"Agent Pippin, I think rescind covers your meaning better."

"Keep playing Scrabble with me, motherfucker, and I hope when you're eating hillbilly dick in prison it makes it all more fun. Oh, I almost forgot. Your ex-wife was here with a cop. She wanted to give you this in person."

He handed me a paper and stepped off the porch with a jaunty strut to the car. He looked too dapper for my working-class neighborhood in his crème-colored suit and charcoal tie. The truth was, I envied him. I envied every simple man on my street who lived a normal life.

"Hey, you haven't asked me what I think of niggers yet," I shouted.

He threw me the finger without turning around. I was down to less than a couple hours to move some pieces. Pippin wasn't the only one who had time pressing at his back. I was a third-string utility infielder at bat in the ninth inning with two hits. I wasn't looking for a homerun or even a single. All I wanted was to turn away from the fastball in time, let it screw into my kidneys and hope I didn't piss too much blood afterward.

I checked out back in the shrubbery and inside the garage and behind it. I saw the hoof prints of a deer and some scat where it had lain down the night before. The grapevine was crushed flat. I went back inside, checking upstairs and down looking for anything obvious. If the place was bugged, and I had to believe it was, I'd never find anything without sweeping equipment better than what I could afford at Radio Shack. I checked the views from the windows in case Pippin's timing was meant to distract me so his agents could move into place.

It was already five minutes to one. I had to get the walkie-talkie from the attic and make the call to Marija. I had to pack a suitcase of clean clothes. I was now officially homeless. Sarah had included a restraining order in my eviction. All that water-logged money sunk to the bottom of an old man's swimming pool and not a dollar of it could help me now.

#14

I found her in the booth of the Oak Room right on time. She might not have been tailed in the holiday crowds out on the street, but I knew we both would be once we left the bar. I sat down across from her and saw the drink waiting for me. She gave me a greeting, as if surprised to see me, and when I slid into the booth, she got up and came around to embrace me. She gave me a passionate kiss with her tongue moving all around in my mouth while her hands moved around my clothes. It wasn't easy controlling my voice after that kind of kiss.

"I take it you've had a lot of practice doing that," I said, but my voice gave me away and she knew it.

"Let's say I've worked with some interesting people in different places," she said.

"Is my drink safe or will I be staggering around outside in the nude telling all my secrets to people in the street?"

"Don't be stupid," she said. "Why would I dope your drink?"

"Why would you take money out of my wallet when I was sleeping?"

"I don't know what you're talking about," she said.

She was wearing a striped top over Capri slacks. Her hair was brushed back over her ears and held there with a headband. Big gold loop earrings and white lipstick made her look like an extra in a sixties' Mamie van Doren film.

"I need to show you something," she said. "Finish your drink."

The crowds streamed around us and she tried to hold my hand as we walked. When we reached the intersection of Little Minnesota, she turned very casually and stopped. She kept her eyes on me but I watched the crowd part in front of us and fold back together.

"Do you see the old arcade across the street?"

"Yes, I do. It's abandoned."

"See the padlock on the front door?"

"I can't see anything. Too many people," I said.

"Never mind. It's there but it doesn't work. Come down that side of the street walking east with the money. When you get in front of the arcade, wait for the crowd to build up a little and then push the door open."

"Will you be inside?"

"I'll be standing out front. If you walk past me, I turn around, and your brother dies. If you try to set me up, I'll walk away from it. There's nothing to link me to any of this," she said.

"Will my brother be inside?"

"Just do what you're told and stop asking questions. Keep the walkie-talkie with you from now on. We want to know where you are every second."

I said, "We can meet somewhere isolated and I can hand it to him. We don't need to do this James Bond stuff out in the open like this. Too many people. We'll be covered in cops, Marija. It's too complicated."

"He doesn't trust you," she said. Then she thought a second and smiled at me again with her pretty teeth. "He doesn't trust me either. It has to be right here in this crowd. He knows the cops are watching you. He's watching you too."

"I'll need to see my brother before I hand it to you. No brother, no money. It's that simple. Tell him that."

"I'll tell him," she said. "But I can't promise. He's paranoid. Just follow his instructions," she said. "Your brother and you can come out of this alive. It's the only way."

"How do you know he isn't going to dump you and run off with the money?"

"I'll worry about me," she said and gave me that incandescent smile she kept in reserve. She held out her hand for me to shake. I felt the paper slip lightly from her hand to mine.

"I'll call your home phone tonight and tell you why we're not a compatible couple after all," she said. Who was she, this woman? I wondered. Some men actually stopped to look at her. She was a chameleon. I was a sap and way out of my depth.

"You won't have to try hard, Marija," I said, but she'd never hear me above the crowd and the traffic. An orange Stingray drove by with its chassis outlined in purple neon, and I saw the driver's head swivel to take her in as she passed in front of him.

I stood there feeling the press of human bodies moving all around me – people in singles and pairs, groups of four and five, all chattering happily. All the younger ones had cell phones and were carrying on animated conversations. Living in two worlds. I wasn't comfortable anywhere.

I had to call Stevie, the cabbie, right away about the drop location. A scrap of information floated up to my brain. I looked once more at the boards nailed over the windows of the old penny arcade. It contained ancient amusements from the 1950s but had finally lost its nostalgia value to the babyboomers and gone bust. The last time Sarah and I walked around inside its dusty interior, I saw the same quarter machines where tiny metal buckets clawed in brightly colored rubble for packets of gum and cheap toys stamped made-in-Japan behind the glass. I fed quarters into a machine that returned postcard snapshots of women in bathing suits. Most of them had chubby thighs and would have looked matronly on a modern beach filled with young beauties.

I crossed the street and walked by it. The last owner had installed glass block windows in some belated effort to achieve shabby chic. Some of the blocks were smashed in or missing. The big front glass panes were smeared with white stain.

I walked down the sidewalk to the back of the building

and felt the hackles of my neck rise at the thought of Calderone out there watching me. He'd have to be crazy to hang his face out in public. Then I remembered what Pippin said about him. Out behind the building I saw the door had a similar rusty padlock hanging from it like the one in the front. It wasn't a perfect place, way too much in the open, but I didn't have a choice.

I drove to Erieview and asked to see the manager's cabin. He was delighted that someone wanted to rent a cottage after Labor Day, and I had my pick of places. They were named for famous lakes all over the world. I chose Lake Winnipeg. The old man had actually driven us there once for vacation so it might be lucky. Maybe that's why I had lakes on the brain. I was born in a state that had bragging rights for a thousand of them. At least that's what my father told me when I asked why we didn't speak French like everyone else in Montreal.

It smelled of mildew and disinfectant. There were aged photos on the walls of steamships in winter and summer scenes. Many of them were taken at the Soo locks and Superior, Wisconsin. I saw a sepia-tinted photo in the bathroom of one of the original steam vessels contracted by Carnegie to haul his iron ore from Minnesota fields. It had a stovepipe stack with guy wires holding it in place on the boat deck. It didn't look like something you'd want to be on in a winter gale.

I paid the manager for three days. Now I was down to forty-five dollars. Rick the prick had left the gas tank on empty for me so there wouldn't be much left by the time I got back.

#15

I pulled the truck into Emil Danko's driveway, not sure whether I'd get past the eagle-eyed old Korean War veteran.

I knocked on his door and waited a long time. I repeated the knock loudly enough to rattle the colored glass panes and heard his wheelchair motor approaching. He was muttering something to himself as he opened the door. He looked at me a long time, blinked twice, and then he recognized me.

I saluted. "Congratulations, Sergeant Danko, First Marine Division, X Corps."

"Congrat for what? Say what? Say, ain't you that same

guy was here last week pokin' around my place?"

"You've been nominated by American Foreign Legion Post one-one-five-oh as its candidate to put forward for national selection as one of the top ten veterans of foreign wars. Combat magazine sent me to do a feature story, and I just have a few questions for you..."

My spiel was borne of desperation. I was careering into absurdity from every angle, and if my mark were less pathetic than a senile old man in a wheelchair, I'd have given up all hope. As it was, the forces of darkness were still pitching a shutout.

But as I mumbled through the last portion of this nonsense, he wheeled aside to let me in. From then on, he never left my side. I pretended to take copious notes. Mostly I wrote obscenities about luck and fate, doodling after each response to a question. Danko had those times, dates, and names locked into a part of his brain that had somehow remained diamond-sharp. The frozen Korean peninsula and the Chosin Reservoir remained for him a timeless, never fading tower planted deep in his neocortex despite the crumbling edifices time wrought on everything else before or since.

After fifteen minutes of this, I asked him if he still used the swimming pool out back. He stopped in mid-sentence, looked perplexed for a moment, back in some distant siege when the Chinese infantry came pouring out of the ravine and pinned his unit down into the frozen earth. He recovered, however, and said he had it installed for his grandkids and was still paying the damned thing off. They hadn't used it in two years, he mentioned. He was revving up for a return to his war story when I interrupted him again with a request:

"Would you mind, sir, if I took a quick look? I'm thinking of getting one just like it for my own kids."

"You don't want to do that now," he huffed.

"Why not?"

"It's all dirty and full of that... that green shit, bacteria big as my head."

I left him sitting there with his mouth agape and walked through the back of the house to the back door. I heard the whine of his motor as he tried to catch up with me.

I slammed the door behind me and went to the pool. I untied one of the flaps. He was right: the surface water oozed with a green scum, and it smelled very bad; the stench of the black, stagnant water overpowering under the closed pool cover.

I hopped over the side at the shallow end. I waded through the viscous liquid from my knees to my waist while my head stretched the top of the vinyl cover. I dog-paddled to the deep end where I remembered tossing in the heavy canvas bags.

I dove under and swam to the bottom; my ears stung immediately from the sudden pressure change. I used the slimy pool side to guide me down to the murky depths and patted the vinyl bottom in all directions. Nothing. I came up and tried to remember where exactly I was when I tossed them over the side. I was sucking in air for the third dive when my treading foot kicked something. I reached down and felt the matted fur of an animal's carcass. It could have been a raccoon that fell in. I took in another lungful of air and went down. I combed the bottom with my hands and legs against the buoyancy pulling me back up. It was like swimming in urine; my eyes burned with the pool's supercharged acidity from years of neglect.

Then I touched something and groped along it until my fingers found it. I hauled it up. It weighed a ton. I couldn't swing it over the side. My feet had no purchase in the slippery pool bottom. I inched my way back to the shallow end, gasping, and threw the bag over where I had entered the pool.

I went back to the place where I had found the first bag and dove in again. I did this three more times and came up empty-handed. Every muscle in my body ached and my eyes burned from the filth. I was almost blind. But I found it on the fourth try. When I climbed out after it, I lay gasping in the grass and blowing hard out of my mouth. I vomited up some bile and dirty water.

I knew Danko was watching me the entire time, from one of the tiny slats of his kitchen window. Because of his wheelchair, he was unable to get close enough to the back door steps to see what I was bringing out of his pool, but he could hear me gasping and thrashing in the water easily enough. I got up and walked to the window. On my tiptoes, I could see part of him through the shadow. His mouth hadn't closed much. He was spluttering as if he too had taken in mouthfuls of rotten muck.

"You... you... you're crazy, man! You'll get sick and I'm not paying for your medical if anything-"

"That's all right, Sergeant, stand down. I'm fully covered for these emergencies." My ears popped like firecrackers. I looked up at his pale reflection in the window. It was hard to see his face through my bleary, reddened vision.

"May I have a glass of water to wash out my eyes?"

"Get off my property, you crazy lunatic!" he screamed.

I heard the high-pitched whine of his motor, like bees trapped in a jar, as he retreated deeper into the recesses of his house where pool-diving maniacs like me couldn't reach him.

I gathered up the bags and walked back to the truck. The water squished out of my clothes and poured from the tiny holes at the zippered ends of the bags, failed levees for the tidal surge, but I hoped the two layers had kept the money from being completely contaminated.

As I threw them into the passenger side of the truck, I saw the curtains swishing back and forth in Danko's living room. I had to paw my way around the truck fender to get into the driver's side because opening my eyes for more than a couple seconds was too painful. I couldn't waste time looking for a garden house to wash them out. The stench of rotting eggs and whatever else comprised the effluvia of Danko's pool was enough to gag generations of maggots. I was just about to climb in when I heard a soft, feminine voice behind me.

"You're Jack Trichaud," she said.

I turned around and saw the grim-faced lover of Alicia Fox-Whitcomb staring at me. "Jack Trichaud, blackmailer," she said. Her eyes were wide open. My grotesque appearance must have caught her off-guard.

"You disgusting, lying piece-of-shit," she said.

"That's me, for sure," I said.

She had those tiny distended white lines around the mouth that Sarah developed whenever she was angry. My ears were still ringing but I heard a low noise like a cat growling deep in its belly.

"So now you're over here tormenting a harmless old man."

"I can't explain. You'll have to trust me."

"Trust you? Trust you? You lowlife bastard..."

Her invective went on for a while. She had a so-so cussing vocabulary. Her eyes flashed and her fists were clenched, but it was all so dreary to me right then, I just wanted to leave, go somewhere, get clean. I was an unemployed actor stumbling from the set of a bad fifties vampire movie to the Creature from the Black Lagoon.

"You're right, you're right, I am all of those things and worse. But right now that old man is calling the police on me and it'll come out, you and her, your marriages will be over, so I have to go right now..."

"I hope you catch the Ebola virus, you fucker. What were you doing in that pool?"

"I'm really very sorry," I said and climbed into the truck. I turned the key and looked at her. She stepped closer and signaled me to roll down the window. She spat into my face.

"You wait until my husband gets home, bastard. You just fucking wait," she snarled.

"Tell Alicia, I'm sorry," I said. I wiped spittle from my chin with my sleeve. "Tell her I never wanted her to hurt either of you. Thank her for not... talking to the police."

"You miserable sack of dog shit. Go back into the sewer you just crawled out of. When my husband gets home, you're going to die screaming in your blood!"

Her cursing was picking up a little but that last was too

Grand Guignol for me, so I peeled out, tires squealing. A last glimpse of her in the rearview showed her giving me the finger. It was more antic farce in one week than most people would experience in a lifetime. After nine years of middle-class tranquility, this non-stop lunacy had me questioning my sanity. I caught another look at my face and was shocked by the appearance; think the before-and-after mug shots of a meth addict. My sunlit dive into Danko's Stygian abyss had left me with bloodshot eyes, looking like a man with a diseased soul wearing its hideous image on my face.

It wasn't any consolation, but I thought Alicia's lover's husband would have to get in line. First, I had to wash out my eyes and get the primordial stench off me. Even Calderone's roofer couldn't have smelled this bad when they dug him up.

I drove to a BP gas station and walked up to the boy behind the glass cubicle. He looked at me with wide eyes. If I had asked him for all his drawer cash, I suspect he would have forked it over with the washroom key. I got as much crud off me as possible with the industrial-strength soap and belched up a rancid gaseous bubble.

It was barely tolerable driving even with the windows down. My blurred vision had me weaving all over the road.

Watching out for cops, I managed to catch a glimpse of a pair of older SUVs, tailing me front and back in a tight box. I cursed my life, my brother, my father's seed all the way back to the Book of Deuteronomy. I wondered what lunatic fairy had presided over my birth to give me this mixed-up life.

I joined the crawl-speed traffic on the Strip and headed

toward Erieview.

No pedestrians were about but crowds were beginning to gather on the streets for the night life. I stopped in front of my cottage. I held off my desire to race into the shower. The swinging placard with the burned letters of Lake Winnipeg swayed in the gentle breeze off the open water. It was going to be a steamy hot evening, another fluke of weather this late in the year, and a full moon rising. I had no choice. If Pippin – or worse come to worst, Calderone with an axe in his hands – was waiting for me, what was I going to do? I was too fatalistic just then to care.

I hauled the bags out and unlocked the door – nothing but the gloomy emptiness of its space and ancient cigarette smoke.

My father taught me stillness. How to stand in a room and feel the molecules of energy tell you who was hiding inside or who had been there before you. You can tell, he said, whether they were friend or foe. He called it using the 'dog brain.' A person smells pizza in a nearby house, a dog's nose can separate the cheese from the pepperoni. It's like the 'cancer' scent some people give off, a whiff of putrefaction from the cells' mortal struggle.

The scents I ferreted out were nothing compared to my body's noxious aroma. I showered for an hour and scrubbed myself raw. Pippin would expect me to use a cell phone and use the tower pings against me in court, but I don't own a cell phone and he couldn't get a tap on the pay phone on Erieview this fast, or so I hoped. Raging paranoia, to me, was normal behavior in my growing-up years.

I set the dampest of the money packets out to dry all

over the room. Most of the binding wrappers had come loose so the money was in scattered denominations. I scrubbed my hands with cleanser after touching the bills; this money would remain foul-smelling for a long time.

I shoved the rest of it back into the canvas bags and looped them together with a rope I took from Rick's truck. The cottage across the small alley from me was having a pool dug out. I tied one end off with a clove hitch to a piece of rebar sticking out of the hole and dropped the bags over the edge into a wind-stunted bush growing out of the cliff.

#16

The strip was jammed with people and noise. Mostly the younger crowd beginning to reclaim the night spots for drinking and cruising for sex. I had twenty minutes to kill before the exchange. I tried to keep my mind empty and passive.

The walkie-talkie stuck out of my windbreaker pocket. I could have had a hundred agents trailing me. Pippin had to be out there somewhere. I was walking around under the eyes and claws of a lot of cats waiting to spring, but I was more like the cheese than the mouse, the bait to bring Calderone out of the shadows. I knew without Pippin telling me, whatever snafu had landed him in Youngstown, this capture would launch him into a plum assignment in his choice of field offices. He had no other reason to let me walk around except for that.

Once in a while the old man would trot out a bible quote, too: 'Pride goeth before destruction. A haughty spirit before a fall.' Beware your own pride, Agent Pippin, I thought as I walked along, just another middle-aged tourist on the Strip. In the foreground of my thoughts was how Calderone was going to come at me. Rick's truck had a few heavy tools lying in the bed, but I dismissed that as foolish. Bringing anything short of a howitzer would be a mistake. Calderone wouldn't let himself get trapped at the money drop, when he knew I'd come trailing FBI agents like a string of picnic ants. Pippin, as SAC of this op, could have called out dozens of agents to have this town thoroughly combed – every rock on the beach and every tree in the state park north of here. The papers said less each day as the news of the crime faded from the headlines.

Finally, I gathered up the shreds of my courage and headed toward Little Minnesota. A couple runaways were soliciting change, a come-on for a different kind of transaction if you were a single male walking alone. But neither of the girls bothered me as I crossed the street to the arcade.

I walked down the length of the sidewalk next to the arcade and felt the heat rising from my neck. A few more feet would determine whether Stevie and her friend had managed it...

I turned the corner. I spotted it at once: big and green and topped up with some real garbage bags for effect. My legs almost buckled with relief. I had just enough time to get back to the cottage for Marija's call.

I reached Erieview when I heard the outside phone ringing. My watch said I was on time, but she was calling three minutes early.

I reached it a few seconds after the last ring.

"That was the last tenth ring," she said. "If you hadn't picked up, I was going to hang up, and your brother would start arriving in tomorrow's mail – a different piece every day."

"You don't have to threaten me, Marija," I said. "I'm cooperating."

"The next part is real important, Jack."

"Just tell me what I need to know," I said but my hand was shaking on the receiver.

"All right, you're upset. I can understand that."

"Your empathy astonishes me. Get to it."

"This is all up to you now. If you make any mistakes – if you deviate from one instruction I am going to give you by even a fraction – your brother's life is over. Take longer than each task allows for, and he dies."

"Before you give me what you call these tasks, tell me one thing."

"You don't have much time for this..."

"Just tell me-"

"Jack, shut up. There's nothing left to do but obey."

And that's when I was convinced I was going to be killed. I imagined my father assessing the situation coldly. That's what he would have recommended standing in Randall's shoes.

"Ready?" she asked.

"Let's get this over with," I said.

She made me repeat things. It was meticulously detailed. I think my father would have approved.

"You've given me a lot to remember," I said.

"You can handle it," she cooed, "especially the inside parts. We're watching you. Maybe not every second, but you won't know when we're not."

I checked my watch.

"Start walking," she said.

#17

My first stop was the Oak Room, where I sat at the bar for thirteen minutes precisely. I ordered and drank a sidecar. My next stop was the Sunken Bar. It was on the same side of the street but it was back the way I had come about five-hundred yards. The same thing: order a certain mixed drink. Leave at precisely a quarter after the hour. Cross the street and enter the Cove, which was a bar for the younger crowd.

I had a hard time attracting any of the three bartenders because of my age. The music was loud, new wave, irksome. The bartender didn't know how to make a sidecar so I ordered a dry martini. That also sent a pained expression across his face. I asked him what he could make with Jack Daniels. "Shot-and-beer," he said. I was down to five minutes.

On the way with my drink, he stopped to chat with a girl at the other end of the long bar, and I lost more time. I threw a five down, bolted the drink, and was off my stool running before he could finish asking me if I wanted another.

This wasn't about checking for tails. It was about getting me shitfaced so I'd be too docile to put up any resistance. I had one more bar to hit at the end of the Strip. I was feeling the effects of blitz drinking by the time I opened the door of Rita's and walked into the soggy gloom, the booze was making me dizzy and my skin tingled. I had less than twenty minutes to get there and down a couple beers.

The bartender was the same one I had seen the first time with the gold-loop pirate earring. When I ordered two beers, he popped the tops on two Budweiser cans and slid one to me. I had the first one halfway down, when he slid a shot in front of me. I saw him holding a bottle of by the neck.

"Johnny Walker Red," he said. He set a red plastic cup in front of me.

"I don't want that," I said.

"I was told to give it to you by a woman friend of yours. She said you'd try to refuse but you'd understand. All one to me, man."

"I'll double whatever she gave you to say I drank it," I said and started to fumble for my wallet.

"One hundred," he said and waited for me to put up.

I couldn't afford it, and he muttered "bullshitter" and walked off.

It was a double shot and I was already light-headed and oozing sweat. I threw it back and waited for it to hit bottom. I looked at the beer and checked my watch. I had three minutes and twenty-two seconds to get this down. I had to be at the pay phone on the corner of Little Minnesota. I took it down in three swallows and waited for it to settle in there with the hard booze. I had been drunk on boilermakers once before. It was a mistake I told myself I'd never repeat. I was trying to will myself into shape for the next beer when my arm was jostled by someone sitting next to me.

"Like another beer, Jack?" Marija said.

"No, thanks. I'm good." You evil cunt, I thought.

My fingers twitched at the thought of grabbing her by her blonde hair and smashing her lovely face into the bar hard enough to leave teeth embedded in the wood.

She waved the bartender over and set a fifty on the counter. "One more for the road for my friend – same thing," she said. He brought me a beer and another red cup topped up with amber liquid.

"What happened to your eyes?" she asked. "They're all puffy."

"I've been crying," I said. Looking at that cup, I almost did cry. "I'm not going to be much good to you if I'm passed out in some gutter."

"I want you," she said slowly, "to do exactly what I told you to do or you'll never see-"

I drank the shot and chased it in one long swallow with the beer. It burned like acid.

"Keep the walkie-talkie on," she said and got off the stool. I now had less than a minute and thirteen seconds to get to that pay phone.

She threw something in my lap.

I watched her go. I took the last money I had in my wallet – the last I had to my name – and I set it on the bar. Where I was going, money wasn't going to be useful.

When I came out of that cave-like dark into the mellow light of late afternoon, I reeled from the shock. I was literally blind for long seconds. My legs were out of sync with my brain, which was a broken gimbal trying to box the compass.

I leaned too far forward and then too far backward. Finally, I was able to open one eye and then the other against the light. I remember colliding with people. I remember being cussed at for a "drunk" and a "jerk." Some fraternity boys grabbed me and spun me around for a little sport but I broke free into a dog-trot.

I had to get that phone and I had seconds to make it. I couldn't focus my eyes on my wristwatch without losing precious seconds.

I lost count of the rings but I finally got my hand on it. Calderone's voice came down the line. "Having a good time, asshole?"

"Not as good a time as I'm... as I'm going to have – when... when I bash your face in," I said. It sounded more convincing in my head.

"That's the booze talking, fuckhead," he said.

"I thought it was me talking to you, asshole."

"Shut up. Turn around and down to the corner where that guy's selling candy apples from a cart. See it?"

"I shee... I see it," I mumbled. I was drunk and scared. Even these low-rent resort cops would pull me aside if they came within feet of my breath or looked into my face.

"He'll give you something. You've got fifteen minutes to fetch the money from your hidey-hole and be in front of the arcade."

"I need... I need more time," I said.

"Fifteen minutes, starting now."

"Where ish- where is...?" I was stuttering into a dead phone.

Candy-apple stand, my brain screamed: Go!

I made for it, my steps ever more uncertain. I was blinking and lurching like a man crossing the Gobi. When the man behind the counter saw me approach, he didn't say anything. He wiped his hands on his dirty apron tied at his waist and reached behind the counter. He pulled out a folded nylon duffel bag and held it out to me.

"Take it," he said.

"Great fuckin' plan here," I slurred.

I took the bag from his hand despite the fact he seemed to be holding it in three places at once. He looked at me with a panicky expression as if I were dangerous as well as drunk.

I thought about finding a water faucet to douse my head. I slapped my face as hard as I could. People stopped walking by to gape or laugh at the drunk. I wanted to scream that I had to get sober fast, blurt that I was walking into a shit storm without a shield.

I staggered toward the arcade, one foot in front of the other like a man learning how to walk on prosthetic legs. People's faces swirled past, my nose was assaulted by honkey-tonk smells, and my stomach revolted at the county-fair smells of cotton candy and dough frying in grease. My burnt-out eyes couldn't take in the bright colors, all jumbled together in the taffy blender that was my brain, so I focused on my walking. The traffic was blasting the air in the street with guitar riffs, stereo booms of rap that overwhelmed strains of twangy steel guitars and mournful country-western laments pouring out of the redneck bars I passed.

Think, concentrate – I made it my mantra. I had to get away from the melee of the crowd, find Erieview, and get the money bags in time.

Somehow my loop-legged canter took me to a restaurant off Times Square where the restrooms had stalls. I stood over a toilet and vomited, which simple act created a spell of giddy laughter; my hands had turned into claws that wouldn't grasp anything.

I slipped to the floor and banged my head against the side of the stall. I had an urge to urinate: everything in life is angles, I said to myself, thinking it sounded profound and hollow at the same time.

Every thought became a rock that I had to push up a hill yet my pinwheel brain refused to obey. "I won't fail you, Carlos," I said to the stranger's reflection in the mirror and stumbled out past several onlookers.

My swollen eyes nearly got me killed crossing the street. I picked my way through a stream of cars, heard horns blasting in my direction, and found myself bent over the hood of a small car that stopped just in time before it sent my kneecaps into my thighs. Lucky for me then I had the drunk's relaxed muscles and so was stunned, not hurt, but the ringing in my ears went up a few more decibels to screech level. The shocked face of the driver made me want to laugh, however. I was two minutes from Erieview. The sweat flew from my head and my clothes were soaked with perspiration.

How I did it, I don't know, but I managed to haul up the bags, nearly pulling up the camouflaging scrub with them, and despite a bearded occupant of the cottage looking out his window at me. The vomiting and sweating must have helped restore some calm to my brain. I transferred the cash into the black bag from the candy-apple man and headed for the arcade.

I was a man on a mission, the duffel bag clutched in a death-grip, oblivious to the stares of the crowds and the distractions all around me. I beelined to the arcade, if you can call a drunken stagger a straight line. Two minutes late.

Marija stood near the curb about ten feet from the arcade's front door. She wore a dark sweat suit and had her hands in her pocket. Even drunk, waxed out of my mind with nerves, I still thrilled to the sight of her and cursed myself. Men, we're all hopeless. Her face took me in at once. She drew out her walkie-talkie and spoke into it.

I bumrushed past her with my shoulder and heard the padlock fly off. I saw the cut marks where it had been sawn through.

"Just like home," I said into the darkness.

I couldn't see anything yet. A voice hissed at me from the black.

"Get away from the fucking doorway," Calderone said. He seemed to be a long way off.

"I can't see you," I said.

At the end of the arcade, a beam of flashlight pinpointed the leg of a chair near the far wall. My heart raced faster than my brain. It was a long descent into the blackness. I hoisted the bags over my shoulder and headed for the light beam.

When I was close enough to hear breathing in the dark, I said, "Carlos."

A light whipped out again. I saw legs and arms, a body wrapped in duct tape.

"That better be money in those bags."

"That probably isn't the dumbest question you've asked today," I said.

The beam of light poked at Carlos, whose face was bruised. His eyelids fluttered. He looked conscious but stoned. It could be fake.

"Give me the bag," he said.

I stopped about ten feet from the voice. The bag dangled from my hand. I let it drop. It hit the floorboards with a smack and shook dust loose. The light beam found it and played over the bag while dust motes traveled in and out of the beam.

"Bring it to me, Jack," Calderone said.

"Kiss my ass."

"You didn't come this far to be stupid."

"I didn't come here to die, either," I said.

"If I wanted you dead..."

"...I'd be dead already. I've seen that film, Calderone."

The absence of light increased my vertigo and made my bravado seem dumber than it must have sounded in this surreal atmosphere. It felt like floating in black air.

The old man's voice penetrated through the booze fog: Control every situation as if your life depended on it.

"How do I know my brother's not dying?"

"How do I know you didn't bring your dirty laundry?"

"Put your light on it," I said. I bent down and unzipped it. I rooted around in it. I riffled a packet of fifties like a deck of cards.

"OK, that's enough. I'll cut him loose."

He played the beam over Carlos' arm, but I saw the glint of the knife he held in his other hand. I felt him moving in the darkness. I'd never get back to the door before he had me.

His voice, a baritone shift to basso-profundo: "I'm going to gut you and wrap the end of your intestines around your neck."

I felt the hiss of the blade near me and I smelled Calderone.

Marija's voice crackled in the blackness: "Someone's coming!"

The light swung back and forth. I heard Calderone grunt as he stabbed the blackness searching for me.

God knows why I took the time to do it, but I did. I bent low and swung my hand toward the floor in the place I had memorized where the straps of the duffel bag were when Calderone's light shone on it. Heavy as it was, I swung it up toward my body in an arc at the same instant I felt a punch to my midsection. The bag took the knife's thrust, but the power of Calderone's blow sent me backwards flying off my feet. I heard the flashlight skitter across the floor.

He swore in a panic. He screamed at Marija, cursed,

and I heard the blade hit the floorboards an inch from my head. His knee had me pinned to floor. I couldn't move his weight and I knew the next blow would not miss. Instead, wanting a sure kill, he launched himself off my chest and went for the flashlight.

My brain screamed at me to run for it. Anybody would have done that – but not anybody had the bizarre upbringing my brother and I had. I rolled five feet away and curled my body into a fetal position with my back to Calderone. I was completely sober at that moment and knew exactly what I was doing. Calderone's hissed curses covered my slightest movements. And his light missed me every time; he thrust it this way and that, cursing violently as it poked a hole in the blackness and I wasn't at the end of it. Seconds were stretched out into spaghetti lengths of time as if I had fallen into a black hole yet I was never more than a few feet from him every time he moved. Sarah had dragged me to the Cleveland ballet once and explained what a *pas de deux* was. In the bizarre way the mind has of doing its own thing, that was what I thought of as I rolled from side to side, listening to the knife stab the floor and Calderone huff from his exertions. I knew I had moments to live.

Marija's voice saved me. I heard her say "FBI" and "cops." That must have broken through Calderone's rage. By then, I was tucked against the wall and folded into as small a space as I could manage with my arms and legs tucked under me, the black duffel bag protecting my neck and head. Even with Marija's hysterical voice warning him, he kept scouring the floor and walls seeking me out. Finally, mercifully, the torch's sweeping arc ceased to probe. It pointed downward at the floor just about five feet from my exposed backside.

Then Marija's whispered hiss: "Coming inside!"

Calderone was rooted to the floor listening as intently for footsteps coming toward him as I had listened for his.

I saw my only chance.

I uncurled my body, came up with the bag in two hands and swung it like a hammer thrower right at the point in the darkness where Calderone's head had to be. The smack of connecting with his head, hearing the grunt, gave me a spurt of adrenalin to my legs and I was running straight for the back wall where the door was – that is, I was running for a spot I had tried to fix in my head as I lay prone waiting for the beam of light to find me. I had the duffel bag in front of me as a buffer in case I misjudged. The padlock, hacksawed through like the one out front, was nothing to stop my momentum. In fact, the entire door blew off its hasps and I was outside on my belly skidding across the gravel on top of the bag like a body surfer in the shallows.

I scrambled to my feet and ran to the green dumpster. I swung the bag over the lip, heard the reverberating thunk of it hitting the bottom, and kept running.

A man came drunk-walking down the sidewalk opposite me. I was terrified he was an undercover cop, but I didn't slow; up close, he looked shabby like a tourist who'd had too much to drink and been rolled. He stopped to stare at me as I bore down on him and I saw the fearful look on his face.

The rest is largely a blank. Bless you, Stevie, I thought. I do remember thanking her for the dumpster.

I circled back to my cottage through back alleys and twisting paths.

As I was putting the key into the lock, all the tension, joy, and fear were colliding in me in the aftermath of my escape, when the door opened of its own accord, and I knew then I was fucked.

When I came to, I was on the floor in a different cabin and Randall Calderone was sitting in a chair talking calmly into a walkie-talkie. When he noticed me awake, he shifted in his chair just enough to plant his boot on my chin.

"You know I'm going to kill you, right?" He said it without malice or pleasure, and as I was thinking that odd, his boot came down hard on the point of my chin and this time the blackness swallowed me whole. Daylight opened my eyes for me and I finally regurgitated all that was left of the alcohol and fear in my stomach.

#18

I managed to roll myself into an upright position. My hands and feet were laced together with a nylon cord.

I coughed some of the rheumy phlegm up from the back of my throat.

Calderone was oiling an automatic.

"That for me?" I asked.

He barely turned his head to acknowledge me.

"Where's my brother?"

"Marija scored some shit. He's zoned out."

"You mean a hot shot? Is he dead?"

A sibilant hiss of static air came over his walkie-talkie. I leaned my back against the wall and tried to ease some of the pressure from my aching wrists.

For a split-second, I was terrified Calderone had recovered the money. That was the only reason I was still alive.

He was bare-chested and had a bottle of Jack Daniels on the table in front of him. Two glasses, one with lipstick stains on the rim. Besides the gun-cleaning equipment on the table, he had a Bowie knife and a cell phone. This cottage had Norman Rockwell prints. I didn't know if we were close to my cottage or whether I had been moved while unconscious.

Then it clicked: They couldn't get near the money in that dumpster. Too many cops around...

"You remind me of some guys in the joint," Calderone said. His voice made me jump. I couldn't imagine what my brother's fear must have been like when he walked into his cell and found this psychopathic ape glaring at him. "The ones like you, Jack. The ones liked the sound of their own voices too much. I enjoyed breaking them up the most."

"Go get the money if you know where it is, Calderone."

"If you don't want the yellow shit stomped out of you, you'll be quiet now."

"Trying to be useful," I said.

"That FBI agent, the nigger that's been hanging around you, he isn't looking at the arcade," Calderone said. "But Marija's got cops all over her sweet little ass."

"I just want to get my brother and me out of this," I said, but it came out of me like a squeak. I had no courage left. My father's bag of tricks was all used up.

"Who said you or your bro are getting out, fucker?" He gave me the wide-open grin up to his canines. It wasn't comforting.

I asked him for a drink of water and that merely earned a response to the effect that my front teeth would be kicked into my stomach if I repeated the request.

Ten minutes later, Marija called on the cell. Calderone listened but said few words back. I gleaned this much: Rick reported his truck stolen and it was towed off.

"Pippin thinks I can lead him to you," I said. "You just made his job easier."

Calderone didn't use his boot this time, but the backhand had some zest in it. I couldn't wipe bloody drool off my chin. This wasn't how it went in the movies.

"Your FBI nigger," he said, "he sees you walking around, what's he gonna think?"

"I kept my end of the deal," I said. "What do you gain if you kill me?"

"Satisfaction," Randall said. "I like it. It gets me hard."

He got up, stood in front of me and rested his boot sole against my cheek and pressed my head backward into the wall until my face twisted into a grimace of pain.

"Like that, Jack. I like that look."

He picked up the walkie-talkie from the table and spoke into it. I heard "choppers," I assumed he meant helicopters, not false teeth or Harleys.

Then, very clearly, indifferent to what I might learn, he barked into the phone: "Give him whatever the fuck you got, bitch. Who gives a shit now?"

I knew Carlos was alive and he was with Marija, wherever that was.

How long could nine-hundred thousand bucks sit in a dumpster before the FBI, the cops, Calderone or Marija –

maybe even one of the resort's dumpster-divers – found it?

I saw the wolf grin appear on his face as he turned to check on me.

If you run with wolves, don't trip. Another saying of the old man's, another lesson I had failed to learn well until it was too late.

Two weeks ago I had seen it coming apart at the seams, but it was in another house in a different county: Alicia Fox-Whitcomb's house. Instead of being surrounded by her loving husband and daughter, she had three strange men holding her hostage, everyone waiting for the bank to open...

TWO WEEKS AGO

MONDAY, AUGUST 16

3:03 A.M.

"BANK DAY"

#19

I woke in the middle of the night with my same nightmare: the hail pelting me senseless and every chip of ice drew blood. I leaked like a sieve and stumbled from one side of the road to the other. Then I discovered a shovel in my hand and started looking for a place to dig a shelter. I was alone.

The hallway was black but there was a thin light beneath the door of the master bedroom at the end of the hallway. I walked toward it and looked in. I didn't have to see him to smell him. Randall was asleep in there among the black formless shapes. I remembered how he had crept up on me that first time. I heard the sound of his deep breathing and relaxed.

I leaned over the staircase and saw Alicia's husband David slumped in his chair. Brandi, the daughter, and her boyfriend were nestled into each other as well as their handcuffs permitted. The boy used his body like a shield for hers. I saw her foot twitch in nervous sleep.

I was a few steps from the boyfriend's head when I saw him twist his neck to look up at me. He stared, confused at first, and then his pale features assumed the rigid look of hatred.

Carlos had left sufficient light to see around the room but only enough to make it look from the outside like a house asleep for the night. I leaned farther over the banister and picked up the sound of his voice from the kitchen – an urgent sort of whispering, conspiratorial but something else, too, friendly like, as if two intimates of a household were stealing a few minutes together for a midnight snack or a close chat.

I couldn't hear what he was saying. Drugs were keeping him high. I walked back up the steps, dragging myself, my bones aching with every step. I went into the small bathroom near Brandi's room, put the light on and immediately shut it off. The glare was painful. I had bouts of insomnia before but they were always connected to Montreal. My body and my mind were both exhausted, crossing wires indiscriminately. I splashed cold water on my face and looked at the changes in the mirror. Domestic life and a laboring job had put twenty-five pounds on my frame since my hitchhike up to Northtown. Now I was going backwards. The environment, time, and my body were collapsing in at once. I returned to Brandi's room and put her pillow over my head. The scent of her on the pillow was strong.

I closed my eyes and let the dark have what was left of my consciousness. At one point I remember jolting upright in the bed because I thought Randall was standing in the room with that butterfly knife in his hand. He had come to do what he promised. I lay back down and waited for the light in the window to change to smoky grey.

Downstairs, Brandi and Brad exchanged a look as I stepped around them. One end of the duct tape covering David's face had slipped down. He looked at me but I didn't meet his eyes as I replaced it over his mouth. Even in the poor light of early morning, I could see their red-rimmed eyes and haggard faces and knew sleep had been impossible for all of them.

I walked into the kitchen and saw my brother still talking to Alicia. They seemed to be frozen in place.

"Have you slept?" I asked her.

"She's doing fine, just fine," Carlos said cheerily.

"I wasn't speaking to you," I said and poured myself a cup of coffee.

She wouldn't look at me. I suppose she kept featuring me as the nitwitted yard man and couldn't reconcile me with this other, darker persona. I looked at Carlos and wondered what loony charm he exuded to dispel the notion that he was any less responsible than I for the brutalizing of her family. In the deepest cockles of my heart, I admired her. She didn't whine about the injustice of what we were doing. She was wise to avoid making a fuss. Randall was playing second fiddle to my brother, who gave off too much kinetic energy. At that moment, I was worried myself. He was a different creature in this house than he had been in mine. As repulsive as he was, a little antic buffoonery from him would have put my mind at ease. A somber, purposeful maniac is a scary one.

"Change of plans," Carlos said. "You're going with her."

I stared at him. It wasn't the constant improvising that appalled me. It was the fact he was telling me this right across the table from her.

"Let's talk over here," I said.

Carlos apologized profusely to Alicia for having to handcuff her to the cupboard handle but she didn't seem to mind. We walked into the den.

"Where's Randall?" I asked him. "What's he saying to your change of plans?"

"Relax, Jack, will you? It's all right. Look, that fucking FBI agent's got a hardon for us right now. He might have alerted cops in this county, too. We can't take a chance by hanging our faces out in front of that bank."

"I don't like this," I said. "This whole dog's breakfast of a plan is insane."

"She knows what to do. Go with her. Sit in the parking lot. Wait for her to come out with the money. Like that. It's over, done." He slapped his hands – presto.

"Jesus, you're really pushing it," I said. "You think because she's listened to your doped-up bullshit all night she's your trained monkey now?"

"Listen to me, Jack. Alicia knows exactly what to say. She's going to walk into her bank with all her staff looking her right in the face and she's going to tell them that three very bad guys are in her house right this second. They will kill her husband, the girl and the boyfriend if she doesn't follow their instructions to the letter."

"You're so sure, are you?"

"Yes, yes, I am, Jack. Because she knows we'll blow up her husband."

"Knows? How does she know that?"

"You mind not shouting so they can hear you across the street?"

"We've all left enough DNA in this house to keep a hundred crime-scene technicians busy. Do you think you're just going to fade away with bags of money?"

"Yeah, like fade into Bolivian," Randall said behind me so close I felt the hackles on my neck rise.

I never heard him come down the steps but Carlos did and never gave him away with his eyes. That's how they must have done it in prison when somebody was about to get sucker-punched.

Randall whispered softly in my ear like a lover: "That's what we're all going to do right after the split."

"It's settled," Carlos said. "You go with her."

"We're trusting you, Jack," Calderone said. He looped one of the blue duffel bags over my shoulder and handed me a walkie-talkie. "But not that much, see?"

She reversed her Lexus out of the driveway and waited for my brother to finish giving me instructions. Randall got in the Jeep. He would stay with her until we made it to the bank and then he was going to be in contact. My van brought up the rear. "Don't climb up my ass with this thing, either. If I have to stop her, I'll need some room."

He leaned in the window and gave me the full benefit of his sour breath. "Keep it on that channel. You move it off three and you'll pull back a bloody stump next time I see you."

I asked him what was wrong with cell phones.

"You want to take a chance on a dropped call at this point, dummy?"

"Won't this chatter get picked up by every two-way in the area?"

"Not these babies. We got special crystals cut for them. Cops and taxis won't be able to pick us up. You got any more questions – shove them up your ass, motherfucker."

A quip about his finesse in the teaching arts of crime died on my tongue. I had faced hunger and cold on my own. I knew the unbearable loneliness of being homeless in big cities with no familiar face passing me by. But the trepidation inside me at that point was like a scalding hot bubble in my stomach. My forehead was either clammy or hot to the touch. I wasn't sure if this was fear acting out through my cells or the onset of a fever brought on by stress and going without food.

She drove her usual way and signaled at every turn. If she wanted to make a run for it, she had only to lose the Jeep in traffic. It had to be going through her mind right at that second: floor it all the way to the police station.

Randall gave Carlos reports at every crossing. He escorted her into the bank's parking lot and did a quick U-turn out so the bank's surveillance cameras wouldn't get much of a look at him. As I passed he signaled me, two fingers to his eyeballs: watch her. I gave him my middle digit and drove around to the back. I put the van in idle and sat far off cater-corner in case I had to floor it to get out fast. Somewhere in my duffel bag, I left a cut-up stocking that was supposed to cover my face. So much for anonymity. She parked in her space and got out at a fast walk. No keys in her hand so she had to be admitted by her secretary. She cut her eyes to me once, fast, and looked away but not before her face wrinkled in one of those ugh-winces.

The door opened and I saw her disappear inside. This was decision time. I drove out front and parked far to the back of the last row in front of Sasha's car. I couldn't see anything inside her bank because of the distance and the drawn blinds across the windows. About thirty seconds later someone drew the blinds up, and my view improved. I saw the shadows of figures and some heads behind the teller windows but nothing else. I put the binocs on the part of the bank where I knew her office was. Too much glare to see very much, just the movement of shadowy figures passing by the window where the thick-plated glass cast off a green glow as if they were underwater. It looked as though all the shapes were heading for her office. I didn't know if this was routine in her bank: did they have to attend a rah-rah session every morning and whoop like Wal-Mart workers?

I heard Carlos' voice crackle beside me. "What's going on, Jack?"

"She's inside. They're inside. I can't see anyone. Nothing's happening."

"Stay cool," he said.

"You're not the tethered goat here," I said.

Five long minutes passed. Then ten minutes passed. Every second was like the tick-tock of doom. I didn't breathe. I had to fight panic. My foot actually touched the gas and my hand went for the gear shift.

Then she came outside.

I put on the stocking mask. A man in a security guard's uniform came out with her. She looked around and saw my van and said something to the guard. She was carrying two canvas bags and he had three in his arms. They were all the same size and buff color and stamped with the bank's logo. He had a gun strapped on his hip. When she got next to my window, I could see he was carrying an automatic instead of a revolver.

I rolled down the window, not taking my eyes from the guard's hands.

"It's too late for a mask, wouldn't you say?"

"It's for him," I said. "Tell him not to get any closer."

"There's eight-hundred-seventy-eight thousand dollars in these bags," she said. "That's all of it. The vault's emptied."

"Put them in," I said. I nodded to the side door.

She gave one of her bags to the guard and thanked him politely and called him Elliott. Then she swung the van door open and dropped in her two bags. She took each one from the guard and tossed them inside the van.

"I don't have to remind you..." I started.

"That's all of it except the coins," she said to me. "You're welcome to come in and check for yourself."

"I was going to say, if there's a single dye pack in there..." I hadn't intended it as an accusation but as a concern about what Calderone might do.

"Your brother told me all about you two," she said. "He's mentally disturbed. That big one, the bald one with the tattoos who doesn't speak or look at me. I know he's dangerous. I'm trusting you to keep my family safe-"

She lost it then and her face collapsed like a wet balloon. Despite the lipstick and mascara, the wrinkles in the corners of her tired eyes were like guy wires stretching her skin to its limit. She looked at me from the darkened hollows of her eyes. She collected herself, a very brave woman.

Then I saw rage. "Do you think I'd risk my family for this money? You disarm that bomb, do you hear me? You make that call, right now!"

She spat in my face. So much for Carlos' talking jag and the Stockholm syndrome. I saw the guard's hand slide up his trouser leg to his holster and I decided not to wait for the rest of her invective. I didn't need it. And I was on the clock. Twenty minutes to disarm the bomb and evacuate the house. That was the deal Carlos made with her.

"Jack, Jack! What's happening?"

"I've got it," I said to him. "I'm leaving now."

"Oh baby, we did it!"

"I'm turning west onto twenty," I said. "Approaching the first intersection at Grolier and Breckensale."

"Take your time, Jackie boy. No speeding – easy does it now."

A few minutes later he asked me for my position again. "Coming up on Vandetter and Demaris," I said. "Still clear. Nobody's behind me."

"Bring those goodie bags home to daddy, you beautiful motherfucker!"

Randall's voice came over harsh and guttural: "...the corner of Paternoster and Randolph, there's some kind of accident with a semi and a gold Camry. Fuckin' cop is on the scene directing traffic. It's still good to go. One lane only. Get in the center lane when you reach Brandywine."

"No traffic tickets, boys," sang Carlos.

"You hear me, fuckface?"

"I hear you," I said.

"Where are you now, Jack?" Meth or crack – whatever he was snorting was taking him to the top of the roller coaster. I was coming up on the last intersection before the city limits. On one corner was an avant-garde art house. Facing it was a Dunkin' Donuts.

"I'm just passing Best Karate Dojo," I said. "Dillon and Eureka."

"Lead him home to me, Randall."

"Carl, shut the fuck up for a second. How much she say?" Randall demanded.

"Eight-seventy-eight," I said.

Carlos' voice came over shrill as a banshee: "O marvelous Jesus, you see now what that lousy week cost us? Two hundred fucking forty, fifty grand! Who knows? Maybe three hundred thou!"

"Shut up. I don't have you in sight yet," Randall said.

"Shit! Cunt! Lying-ass bitch!"

"Shut up, Carl," Randall said. "Where are you, Jack?"

"I'm at the intersection of-"

"I fucking told you we shoulda waited for the Labor Day delivery. No, no, no, you said-"

"-intersection of Maclaverty and Footeville," I said. The names just popped into my head.

"Where the fuck... Jack, over. I don't see you yet. I'm turning down her street right now. You should be close to me."

"-motherfucker, we could have had the whole

goddamned million."

"That's strange," I said, "because I think it's the next street right after Kiss-My-Ass and Fuck-You."

Randall's laugh chilled me deep in the marrow. "Shee-it, Jack. Oh, Jack. You're not doing what I think you're doing, are you? You're not that stupid, are you, Jack?"

"Whoa, whoa, what's this?" Carlos shrieked. "Hey, what's going on? Somebody talk to me!"

I let out a long, deep sigh. It tasted like rotten air that I had been holding inside for what seemed like a month. My neck muscles were still cramped, but I felt all right considering.

"Come in, Jack."

Carlos was spluttering rage; he drowned out Randall's voice.

"Listen to me, both of you," I said.

"Go ahead, Jack. We're listening," Randall said icily. "Carl, you need to shut up, boy. Jack wants to say something."

Carlos was hurling obscenities like verbal mud pies.

"First, I want him off the air," I said. "Just us, Randall."

"Okeydoke. Carl, you hear that?"

"Fuck you! Fuck you! I'll kill you, Jack! I swear to God, I'll kill you!"

"Get him off the air, or I'll toss this walkie-talkie into the next sewer."

Silence.

"Calderone, have you been keeping time?"

"I got us at sixteen minutes and forty-three seconds and counting," he said. He was still calm and I knew I was hearing the prison side of him, the Aryan Brother who dished out beatings and sidled up to people he intended to hurt.

"Then you know she's going to make the call in a little over eighteen minutes."

"Yeah, so? We'll be on the fucking interstate."

"If that bomb isn't defused right now, you and my brother will never see a dime of this money," I said.

"Listen to me now, Jack. That ain't enough time! Carl and me, we gotta get the fuck on the highway."

"I thought the bomb wasn't going to be a real one. Psychological pressure and all that."

"Cut the shit, motherfucker. It had to be a real bomb! You think I'm going to take a chance on a woman spotting a fake and go to fucking jail for fucking life? Carl set the fucking timer when she left the house. That bomb is buying us time to escape-"

"Defuse it or I'm gone for good," I said.

"I can't do that in eighteen – Look, Jack, it's got a boobytrap switch to keep the cops busy for a while. This is Carlos and me now, not you. The cops will have to take their good old time, see?"

"Then you had better gun it straight to wherever you're going. Have a nice life."

"Jack, shit, wait a second, dude! Let's talk about this, motherfucker."

"Start talking to my brother. Give him very precise instructions. If I read in tomorrow's paper that it was disarmed, I'll make contact with you at one o'clock. If not..."

"He's high, Jack. He'll blow up the fuckin' house. You want that?"

"Your problem now," I said. "I don't know what the township police response time is, probably not that much better than the sheriff's, but I'd say you're wasting it."

"Listen to me, you fuckwad. I promise you. Oh, I'm going to make you feel pain like you never knew existed in the world-"

His words scored a path into my neocortex.

#20

The skin of my wrists had turned white around the cords. Calderone hauled me to my feet but I couldn't stand up. I hit the floor so hard I bounced. The circulation in my legs had been cut off too long. His words made no sense at all. I might have been babbling strange words during this incoherence.

I was bound and gagged, ready for slaughter. He was going to make what he had said to me over the walkie-talkie on that day come true and there was nothing I had as leverage to keep it from happening. Being helpless is a strange thing when it happens and when it finally sinks in. Here's the strange part: there's a calm feeling that sneaks in around the corners of terror. It's not denial, exactly. The old man considered himself a pain expert, too. He used to give us examples of people facing death like, say, some guy on a capsized boat treading water in the open sea. He's just waiting for the first shark to hit before he takes a big gulp of salt water and ends it. The amygdala squirts an enzyme, my father said, so that when that shark comes close and you see his big black doll's eyes, you don't feel the pain so terribly. Your brain is getting you ready to die.

So I had a whole different perception of time while I was waiting to die – or, more likely, waiting for the torture to start – and I took a long walk down the various channels of my memory storehouse, secret places I built as a boy to hide me from the crazy reality of my sick world. I have a certain memory: it was one of the coldest Montreal winters I could remember. I see the old man sitting by the window, his hands twitching and fluttering on the arm chair, his brain wiring all shot to rags by then, not even looking out the windows because of the beaded condensation like bat wings. Carlos had been sick all winter with bronchitis and then pneumonia. I stole drugs from a corner pharmacy but it didn't look as if his wasted face would ever come back to life. My father said: "You get caught, boyo, you'll go to adult jail for at least a year."

By then I was responding in kind, half-mocking his delusions. I was dressed to go out into the sub-zero weather, probably looking for something to steal to exchange for food. I was like a mad dog in the streets, breaking into places and selling what I stole to a fence in the harbor. I had been shot at by a rival near rue Cherrier for stealing in his territory.

I kept us alive while the old man succumbed to his phantoms, his brain imploding so fast that he would babble nonsense and wave his hands about. Carlos lived but he looked like one of those skeletons liberated from Auschwitz. He'd lost all his adolescent chubbiness that winter and kept forever the gaunt face I saw when he stood in my kitchen with his pet monster.

The pressure was on me that spring. By then, I was marked out by the municipal police. Nobody ever caught me with swag because they never found any on me. I had just made a good haul in silver from a mansion in the Quai des Brumes, and I was walking through the garden gate when I was spotted. The dogs in the place deceived me. People with guard dogs roaming about don't use silent alarms. My father taught me how to handle my fear and something about dogs that most people never knew. I was so good at hiding fear that the dogs would come right up, tails wagging, while I was stealing their owners' goods. This one cop hated me on sight and never missed a chance to throw me against an alley wall. When I saw him, I ran but I was soon trapped in an alley. I was climbing a rickety fire escape when the bolts snapped and I fell about ten feet to the dumpsters below. I pulled the sack out of my jacket and stuffed it inside one of the garbage bins, rolled off, and started to limp down the alley.

He was waiting for me as I came out. He strip-searched me right there in the freezing cold. He watched me shiver, mocked my shriveled penis. He suspected I'd tossed the stuff into one of the bins, but he wanted to put me away. I had made a fool of him and he was fed up with the taunts from his fellow officers.

He sucker-punched me in the solar plexus and called me some uncomplimentary names. He hated Americans and my French was never more than passable. He wanted to catch me coming back for the silver. I spent one whole night thinking about it, and I told Carlos how I was going to do it. Carlos' eyes lit up with admiration: his daring older brother.

I had to find a way to get Carlos past my betrayal, past my leaving him with our psycho dad, past the dope Calderone and Marija were pumping into him, past all that had happened since then, and get him back to that moment. That, I knew, was the only chance I was going to get.

#21

I heard Calderone yelling into his cell phone, using the words "crazy motherfucker" several times. When he jerked me to my feet again, he threw me backwards on the bed and slashed the cords at my hands and feet with his knife; my legs splayed open. I still couldn't get up no matter what violence he roared at me.

I came to inside the trunk of a car. I was aware that I had been in motion and that the motion stopped. When the trunk lid opened, I saw stars and a crescent moon hovering over Randall's shoulder. I was upside down in a fireman's carry and then dragged, pulled and finally dumped into a lit room. I tried rolling over onto my back, but that required more effort than I was able to make.

"Jesus, Randall, what did you do to him?"

A woman's voice. I would know it forever from somewhere deep in my bones: Marija, blonde hair, succubus, Eurotrash accent, big breasts, betrayer, whore, enemy.

"He looks dead! His face is all black and blue – what did you do to him?" She was shrill, angry. "We might need him to get out of here, moron!"

"Don't fuckin' call me names, cunt." The monster's voice.

The slap that took her on the side of the face must have been a wallop because she flew into the wall and landed hard on the floor. I heard another woman scream.

Randall's deep voice now: "I'm gonna show you two lazy bitches who's running this fuckin' show."

"What about him?" the second woman's voice asked, meaning me.

"Fuck him, he's dead anyway," he said.

#22

When I came to this time, a liquid was going down my throat. My head was being held up. I slopped at the water greedily, lapping it like a dog. The hands that held me were small. A balloon face hovered in front of me and I recognized my brother. I tried to get up but my hands and feet were secured by clothesline.

"Carl, watch him," the other woman said. "I gotta take me a piss."

I think I was a little disappointed I wasn't dead. That blinding light burned me.

"How do you feel, Jack?"

I didn't respond. If I could have spoken, I would have

told him it wasn't worth chewing through the leather straps to be alive.

"Here, drink some more water."

I drank long, blissful draughts of it. It was ambrosia.

"Hell, Jack, go easy," Carlos said. "Water here smells like shit."

I saw the pupils of his eyes. He wasn't as high as I remembered him that day in my kitchen.

"Carlos-"

"Don't talk. Just hearing your voice makes him go crazy," he said.

I suppose I shouldn't have felt anything. I didn't have much in the tank to feel with for one thing, but my brother's betrayal still stung. It got through my battered hide and I was angry. The look on his face registered the truth of it.

"You were fucking around with our money, Jack," he said as if that covered it. I didn't have the words to reply.

"You got nothin' to say to me, man?" Carlos said, as if I were the guilty party. "Not after ditching me in Montreal. Now we're gonna finish this deal and I'm gone. You'll never see me again."

I used every bit of strength I had in my body to reach up to him and grab him. I pulled him down until his face was right in mine.

"The dumpster, Montreal..." I started to say.

"What about the dumpster?"

Randall stood in the doorway with his arm around Marija. Her face was flushed and her eyes had a hard set to them but she hadn't cried. She was holding on to a ripped blouse in front of her heaving chest. Carlos stepped away from me.

"Shit, man," Carlos said, tripping to what I had just said in code for his ears only. He stood up, stepped away, and I didn't see where he went. Ten minutes later, he came out of the bathroom rubbing the inside of his elbow. I stared at him.

"Stupid crankhead motherfucker," Calderone said, entering the room again, "can't you leave that shit alone for five minutes?"

"Jesus," Marija said. "You shot up again."

"Bitch, I'm fine," Carlos shot back. "You suck cock, I like a little crank to mellow me out."

Randall strode forward and his right foot shot up and out and came down like an axe. It caught Carlos on the ear and sent him spinning into the table.

"I'll fucking kill every fucking one of you."

Calderone went berserk. He tore around the room grabbing anyone who came within reach and throwing whatever he touched. Marija went sideways into the wall and dropped next to me. He stomped like a furious child in a temper tantrum. The wings of his nose were whitened and his eyes were narrowed to black holes between his bunched-up facial muscles. Carlos' eyes were glazed with fear.

I was waiting, holding my breath. His chest stopped heaving and his dark, thickened features cleared. He cupped one of Marija's breasts in his hand and bounced it like a baby checking out a new toy.

"Get going," he said to my brother. "When you-all come back, we'll have us a nice little clusterfuck – except for him." Jack Trichaud, designated voyeur. At least I wasn't going to be pummeled into hamburger. Not yet.

He leaned down to me and flashed the blade under my chin and twisted it this way and that to catch the light.

"Change of plans," Randall announced suddenly as if he too were mesmerized by the dancing light flickering off the blade. "We're all going. I ain't trusting none a you motherfuckers alone with that money," he said. "That's fucking that."

I caught the look on Marija's face. If she had been in control before, she wasn't any longer. The sex or rape in the other room, if that's what it was, hadn't made any difference. She looked down at her breasts as if they, too, had had some part in the coup.

#23

Randall's greed, however, won out over his desire to kill me. I now had a viable purpose. Marija was told to bring me along. I knew why as well as she did. I was her boat anchor. Calderone must have feared she might have a secret deal worked out – something she could have cooked up on her own while he was in hiding.

"I'm not getting back in the trunk," I said. We stood outside in the dark beside the Volvo while Randall came out with an armload of guns.

"I don't want you up front with me. You stink," she said.

"Quit fucking around, get in," Calderone said on his way past. He was carrying the big Taurus.

"Strap him in," she said to Calderone. My cords were replaced by nylon cuffs; her ripped blouse by a baggy sweatshirt. The night air was damp.

He trussed me with ankle cuffs and a metal chain around my waist that hog-tied me to the seat. I could move my arms a few inches from my knees.

"If he twitches, shoot him in the balls, you want," he said. He walked off to the others.

"Just look at this once," she said to me. Her purse was open and the black grip of a small gun, maybe a .25 caliber, stuck out. The kind of gun that didn't make holes in you – the kind where the slugs bounced around inside ricocheting off all your organs. "If you see more, it means I'm pulling it out and I will use it on you."

We got in line behind Carlos, with Randall behind us alone in a white beat-up Datsun I hadn't seen before. We drove off with headlights probing the dark. "The Côte d'Azur is beautiful this time of year," I said. "But expensive to live there."

"Fuck you, I won't double-cross him," she said.

"The Treaty of Utrecht was less complicated than this half-assed robbery," I said.

"Shut up, Jack."

"Money does that," I said. "It's like danger. It can be an aphrodisiac to some people."

Carlos was increasing the distance ahead of us. The road was barren of houses out here. I couldn't see any stars above the treeline.

"I wonder what you'll see, Marija, when Mister Big decides it's safe to divvy up the cash. Think you'll see wads of money or the sharp end of that knife he likes to play with?" We both knew my own life expectancy was down to hours and minutes.

"I'm... I'm sorry things turned out this way," she said.

"Your tame creodontus back there is never going to let you or my brother take so much as cab fare. Can't you see that?"

"Creo-what? Is that like a dumbbell? You use a lot of big words for a florist."

"Landscaper," I corrected her. "My father insisted we read a lot of books. Voltaire had some nice things to say about gardening, by the way."

"Randall will never hurt me," she said after a pause. "My family is from Croatia. You need a lot of – I don't know the word. Maybe, stamina – to survive over there."

"You could get a job, Marija," I said. "People here tend to work for a living."

"What fun is there in that? In my country, I'd have to lie on my back all day while some pimp took all the money."

"I see. Randall's more like an equal partner, share and share alike, right?"

"He's what he is. Now shut up, please, and let me drive. He said if you try anything, I am to call him on that walkie-talkie on the seat, and he'll ram the car and drag you off to some tree where he'll skin you alive."

#24

The Lake cops rarely stopped drivers after the bars closed. But it took just one bored cop looking to fill his quota and I had pinned my tiny scrap of hope on that. Randall was packing for a siege. Besides the Taurus I watched him clean and tuck into his pants, I know he had a Beretta with a bobbed hammer stuck in his boot. He had enough high-powered weaponry in his trunk to make a South Bronx gangbanger delirious.

Carlos and I had to memorize gun catalogs for the old man. We committed weapon facts to memory while other kids our age learned math tables. He dragged us to gun shows all over Quebec and quizzed us afterward; a wrong answer meant no supper, two meant a beating. Three meant you better stay out of sight for a couple days.

The table in the farmhouse back there held some serious guns. I saw a Freedom Arms 454 Casull lying next to the Taurus PT 99 that Randall favored. A Savage Model 23 bolt-action rifle lay atop a Smith & Wesson 686 with a four-inch barrel. He had a shoulder-fired assault rifle that looked Czech-made. I couldn't identify it but the banana-shaped magazine of the Uzi was Chinese-manufactured. Just a glance, and I picked out a 1911 Interstar 9mm and a Ruger Security Six in the pile and more boxes of Hornady and Blue Hills ammo than you could count, even a couple of Black Talons and an HP Silvertips – always good if you're looking for a wider wound channel, according to the old man's way of thinking.

"What if something goes wrong?" I asked her. "What if we're stopped?"

She turned her head and gave me a look that said I was better off not asking.

Screwing a monster and killing for a monster were two different things. Sarah owned a gun, a Beretta Jetfire I had bought her for Christmas. I noticed her carrying it to Cleveland when her job required her to travel to the inner city late at night. "I know you can pull it out and point it at someone," I told her, "but if you can't pull the trigger and kill a human being, don't carry it." She left it home from then on.

We turned onto 531 and I knew exactly where the house was situated. I cursed Pippin for not going far enough with his dragnet. The countryside south of Jefferson was littered with back roads dotted with abandoned homesteads and farms that couldn't survive. The sheriff's office spent hundreds of thousands detoxifying meth labs. From here it was a straight shot north three more miles to Jefferson-on-the-Lake.

I thought: This is what a suicide bomber feels like. I didn't have any religion to calm me, and no visions of dancing houris to open my eyeballs to. This was it. My life was coming to an end. I had as much chance as a duck in a Beijing meat market.

"So what's your crystal ball say for my future?" she asked me.

"It says you'll always be a self-centered bitch, Marija."

"It must be your nerves. We're so close to being rich," she said.

I jerked my hands up – I forgot the chain. I wanted to slap the smirk off her face.

The digital glow of the dashboard gave her face a greenish tint. She was looking at me steadily. Her purse was still squeezed next to her against the door.

"I was stupid to think-"

"Think what, Jack?"

"Think you had a weakness..." I couldn't finish it. She was a better pupil for my father than I ever was: find the weakness, exploit it.

"Randall gets a kick out of the fact that your brother is a queer."

"They call them transvestites now," I said.

"You should hear Randall go on about it," she said. "He tells me how hard it is to keep a straight face every time he looks at your brother and thinks of him in a dress."

"I thought he didn't know," I said.

"You underestimated Randall. I never made that mistake," she said.

Carlos was set up before they came to Northtown. It meant I wasn't the only dumb steer in the kill chute. We were within a mile of the Strip and I could barely make out Carlos' headlights. The road narrowed and twisted in S-curves every half mile. I used to worry about Sarah coming home on roads like these in the dark during winter.

We were entering the curve now, and Randall pulled off to wait for us near a side street where the cabins were all rented to bikers. Marija saw Carlos slow down to the posted fifteen m.p.h. Both hands were in a white-knuckled grip on the steering wheel.

"If we see a cop, I'll have to kill you," she said.

"Make it a head shot," I said. "That's all I'm asking."

Carlos turned in to Andy's Grill, which was slotted between the Sunken Bar and the Cove – two of my pit stops from yesterday's trek. All the sidewalk displays and booths were closed down for the night and the workers were finishing their shifts after the customers had gone. Everybody here was a worker in one of the bars, motels, and restaurants lining the strip and belonged on the street or going to their cars. The cops might consider hassling a lone drunk staggering out of a bar at this hour but they knew better than to bother staff or sit in parking lots.

She turned right into an alley that led to a parking lot shared by the Cove and a go-cart track. I saw Carlos dim his lights. They sat there for a few minutes. We sat across from them and waited. Then a woman in her twenties in tight skinny jeans came into view. She joined a knot of teenaged girls leaving Andy's by the side door. They came walking in our direction down the sidewalk. The girls were laughing. They seemed identical in age and appearance – grill workers, fry cooks and waitresses. No doubt they were following in their older sisters' footsteps and probably their mothers' too.

"There she goes," Marija whispered.

"There goes who? Marija, don't tell me this is what I think," I said.

"I love her pussy," she said in a husky whisper. "I wish she'd let me trim her down there."

"Whoever she is, that girl," I said. "Does she know what Calderone is? You just gave her a death sentence when you gave her that little errand. Calderone will kill her."

"Shut up, Jack."

"That is, after he's fucked her brains out and-"

She leaned over and unzipped me; then she dug around until she found what she wanted and began kneading my testicles in a vise-like grip with her fingertips.

"Tell me how it hurts, Jack," she hissed through her teeth. Her face was close into mine and her hazel eyes were as yellow as a badger's. She squeezed again, and I screamed.

"I'll take care of Tanya. But there is no way out for you," she said and flecks of spittle hit me in the mouth. "No way out for you or your stupid little fag brother."

I rocked against the seat back but nothing eased the terrible pressure of her fingertips. I felt as if someone had pulled my spinal cord out of my neck, dipped it in kerosene, and jammed it back in.

"Beg me to kill you," she said.

I made gagging sounds. The cords were cutting my flesh

as I tried to escape the pain.

"I said beg me to kill you and I will," she said.

I begged her and I meant it. She put the barrel of her gun into my temple and pulled the trigger. She pulled it again. The click-click-click of dry-firing sounded like rain on a tin roof.

She checked her watch. "I guess Randall will have to kill you. It's time."

She started the car and drove down the alley and turned left onto the strip. The streets were nearly empty now and there were few people walking. We drove slowly to Little Minnesota, where it was completely deserted except for Carlos' car stopped at the intersection. No cars approached ahead or behind besides us. We pulled up right behind him and stopped.

"Come on, bitch," she whispered.

Then Tanya, the attractive dark-haired girl who had mixed with the gaggle of teens, appeared walking alongside the arcade with the black bag held in her arms like a side of beef.

Jesus, I thought, could she be any more conspicuous? Where were all the damned cops now?

"Come on, come on, hurry up," Marija urged.

Tanya was in no great hurry with her burden. She loped across the intersection toward Carlos and shot a stern, pouty look in Marija's direction, although she couldn't possibly see her through the windshield. "Look at the silly little bitch," Marija said and stiffened in her seat with anxiety. "It's too heavy for her."

The passenger door flung open and she wrestled the bag in. Carlos' arm reached out and pulled the bag inside and Tanya jumped in before the door closed. Marija closed the distance with a tiny squeal of rubber. In the deserted street, it sounded extra loud.

"I've never seen anything so smooth," I said. "All of you should take this on the road and make real money giving fuck-up scenarios for police academies."

"Shut up, Jack," she snapped.

"Remind her to take a shower before you go down on her," I said. "She's been rooting around in all that nasty garbage."

"Talk yourself into some courage because you're going to need it. I'll tell you about some of the things Randall has planned for you on the way back…"

#25

We drove back the way we came without incident – a two-car tandem of thieves, a transvestite, Marija's lesbian lover, who might or might not be innocent, a former landscaper about to become a former human being. What else could I write for my epitaph? Not much, I realized. I was one of life's little people, a loser.

If Marija wanted me to beg for the coup de grâce on the way back, I didn't give her the satisfaction. Pathetic as my life was, I wanted more of it – just simple breathing would do, expelling carbon dioxide and taking on oxygen and nitrogen seemed a blessed gift to me just then. I had one small victory to hope for and that was to get Calderone enraged enough to kill me on my own terms.

She pulled up the long driveway beside a deserted and overgrown apple orchard. I detected a tiny glow of light through the bends in the road as we neared an old farmhouse. Single-storied and swaybacked, it couldn't be seen from the road.

It wasn't until she parked up to the front door that I spotted the kerosene lamp in the front window. Calderone came out and loosened my restraints. I felt the nylon ties at my ankles stretch and split apart as he thrust the knife between them. He had to use a key to undo the waist chain.

He pulled me out of the car by grabbing a fistful of my shirt and said into my face: "I owe you for so many things, I don't know where to begin. Trying to fuck my woman, upsetting me over those people from the bank, stopping me from doin' that little girl's boyfriend, taking off with my money, and in general treating me like shit when I ain't done nothing but right by you by tryin' to put a little money in your pocket. Payback's gonna be one cold dirty bitch, Jack."

He shoved me ahead of him and added a hard kick to my lower back as I stumbled up the rotten steps to get inside. The bag was sitting on the table. Carlos and Tanya were standing nearby. When Randall opened it, he drew back from the stacked bundles of money.

"Whew, what the fuck's that smell?"

"I dropped the money into a swimming pool," I said.

"You dumb fucking-"

"Forget it, baby, we can clean it up later," Marija said. "Money spends no matter what it smells like."

Randall thrust a steel pair of cufflinks on my wrist and cuffed me to the table leg. He said to me, "You so much as twitch, you're gonna get dropped to the floor."

I watched him take the money into the other room. He returned to the women and opened his arms. In his hands he held a couple blue diamond-shaped Viagras. He embraced Marija and this time she let him. He gave her a long passionate kiss, and then he reached out an arm for Tanya, who curled into it. The women kissed him and then kissed each other. Carlos stood there with a nervous smile and eyes pinned. He had shot up during the trip to keep his high.

Then it struck me: the bundles of money on top of the bag were neatly arranged. I hadn't done that. After showing Calderone the bag's contents, I had stuffed the money carelessly back inside and zipped it up. My heart started hammering. I risked a look at Carlos, but I couldn't read his face. During those long minutes when I was Marija's squeeze toy, Carlos could have slipped out of the car and made it to the arcade before Tanya. He had infuriated Calderone yesterday by scoring meth at Little Minnesota with all the cops about. That much I knew because some of those stinging slaps that rocked my head were for 'my dope fiend brother.'

But he might have done something else too, right under Randall's wrathful and suspicious eye.

My instructions to Stevie were to square up the dumpster in front of the glass-paned window. Carlos remembered how I had fooled that Montreal cop Thierry Delorme all those years ago. I had to steal an arc welder, and give myself a crash course in the art of welding to pull it off. The same frigid day I was strip-searched by Delorme I came back at night and broke into the basement of the building. With the cops on stakeout, I cut a hole through the back of the bin and climbed into it for the bag of eighteenth-century silver chalices and trays.

If my drug-crazed brother had decided to do a double-cross, driven by his need for the operation, then once inside the arcade, nothing more than a crowbar was needed to whack out a few glass panes; the bag could have been retrieved from inside through the hole I wanted Stevie's welder to cut. It was supposed to be my ace in the hole, not my brother's. Pippin's men were watching the outside. By the time they figured out the bag of money was missing, it would be too late. I'd have Carlos safe and the money both. That was the plan, anyway, but everybody has a plan before the fight.

All I knew for sure was that once I turned the money over Carlos and I were both dead men walking. It's only at the exchange they can get you, my father said, and he was a past master of dead drops and fallbacks.

If a man isn't distracted while he's having sex with two women, he's never going to be. I looked at Carlos and then at the bag on the table. I stared until he gave me the answer; one glance at the bag told me all I needed.

I mouthed the word "key" to him. Carlos' answer was to lift up his shirt and show me the gun in his pants.

He nodded his head in the direction of their noisy sex: Tanya's clichéd urgings and Randall's guttural noises.

I saw the silver and black Taurus sticking out of his pants. I had to try to keep very still because I felt my body starting to shiver uncontrollably – shock, pain, cold and hunger were taking their toll. I was down to the dregs. The white-hot volts of pain that rippled through me meant I wasn't going to be walking fast much less running.

The most fear I ever felt, the worst spasm of blank desperation that welled up in me like a sob, happened right at that moment. I couldn't look at him. I couldn't bear to see the answer. The dog had returned to his vomit.

The gargling noise from the couch forced me to look. Marija was leaning over Randall's back while he plunged in and out of Tanya with a sucking noise. He had her pinned to the sofa with one hand around her throat and was slamming into her pelvis like a maniac. She had her hands on his forearm and was trying to twist free from the relentless jackhammering. Once she realized he wasn't letting go, she clawed and pulled at his thick arm. It was hopeless. He increased the frenzy of his thrusts into her; his back glistened with sweat. Tanya's eyes opened in terror. Marija had been fondling his sac from between his legs and moved up to watch the agony in her dying lover's face. Her hand slipped between her legs as she masturbated to Tanya's death throes.

"Give her some air," Marija said.

Tanya's hoarse gasping filled the room. It was sickening to hear.

Calderone went back to shoving himself inside her. The slap of skin on skin drowned out her terrified gasps.

"Fuck that pussy, baby. Fuck her good," Marija said. She was a depraved, wild-eyed maenad to his Bacchus.

Tanya went limp, her whole body sagged into the couch, and her hands slipped from Calderone's wrist; one arm dangled at the side of the sofa as he kept pumping.

"Ease off, baby," she said. "Give her some air."

My eyes pleaded with Carlos: Now. He had frozen in place; his face whitened in terror. We were meant to see this psychotic spectacle, the aphrodisiac of death and sex.

He eased off on her throat and the strangled sobs were weaker, not bone-chilling as before. They kept their game going until nothing but tiny whimpers and twitches of her body showed she held on to life.

"Finish her off," Marija said.

Calderone leaned all his weight over Tanya's body now and strained. His arm was stiff and his still-hard penis slid along her pubic ruff. He got off the couch panting with his erection still intact. Marija slid around his knees to engulf his penis and deep-throated him. One hand glided between her legs, which opened and closed to a sucking rhythm. My brother stood mute as Calderone reached his loud climax. If heaven has many windows in a single mansion, hell has even more doors. Tanya was wherever she was, in oblivion, gone from this dimension and as still a witness to their violent orgasms as she had been its catalyst.

"Carlos," I said. "Now."

His hand was shaking. He couldn't do it. He couldn't even draw the gun. He was too stunned by horror to react.

"The gun." I said it louder.

Now they were both looking at us. Calderone's chest heaved from the last spasm, but he understood something was wrong. Marija pivoted on her haunches, her hooded eyes and lips puffy from the fellatio. She had one hand around Calderone's organ like a captured bird.

"What... what the fuck you doin', Carl?" If it weren't for Marija's post-coital fondling, he'd have crossed that space and kicked him through the wall.

"Carlos – the gun, now!" I said.

My brother's stony look didn't change but he took the gun out and slid it across the table to me. It was so mechanical and brazen an act that Calderone was at first stupefied. When he did react, it was with such speed that Marija was knocked out of his path.

I had the gun up, safety thumbed off, in one motion. The shot missed Calderone's head. The arc of my arm swing took my aim high, but it passed close enough to his head before boring through the ceiling rafters that it pinned him to the floor in mid-stride. He looked like one of those brawny Soviet statues in some heroic pose. I adjusted the gun sight to his face; six o'clock was his mouth. My heart and brain flooded with adrenalin. He took a quick step backward at the moment I fired again. Another bullet missed.

"OK, OK, OK," he said. He stood back with his hands raised like useless dinosaur paws in front of his massive chest.

I aimed at Marija. I centered on her left breast.

"Get over there with him," I said.

She stood up and walked over to him.

"Carl," Calderone said. "Carl, what are you doing, bro?"

I pointed the gun back at him and told him to shut up.

"Get the key, Carlos. Find the handcuff key," I said. I kept calm but I was boiling inside.

My brother still hadn't moved.

"You can't go anywhere dragging a table with you, Jack," Marija said.

"Don't say another word because I'm thinking of the

parking lot right now," I said.

"You ain't got the balls to shoot me, Jack," Calderone said. "Any pussy can fire warning shots."

"Those weren't warning shots," I said. "You moved your head." I was silently praying the clip was full and that Randall or his biker pals hadn't been plinking at cans with the ammo.

"All right," Calderone said. "One-fourth. We all get even shares all around."

"Carlos, find the key now!"

He snapped out of it and then he was rummaging in their clothes tossing them behind him like a dog digging in a leaf pile.

I pointed the gun at Calderone's flaccid member still oozing jissom.

"Wait, motherfucker!" Calderone yelled.

"The key, now," I said.

"It ain't in here!" Carlos wailed.

"It's back there in the other room on the window shelf," Calderone said.

Carlos said, "I'll get it." He took off giving the two a wide berth.

"Wait!" I said, but he was already running into the other room.

"You want to think about this, Jack," he said. "We're all in this." He gestured behind him to the prone body of Tanya. "We just have to keep our cool." He lowered his arms to his side. Marija kept her voluptuous body in repose but her face was assessing my nerve.

"He's right," she said. "Look, we're all in this now. Let's think how we can all get what we want-"

"-and go our separate ways?" I finished for her.

"I can't find it!" Carlos hollered from the next room. "No fuckin' key here!"

I could hear him knocking things around in there.

"Jack, why don't we-"

"Shut up," I said.

The noises in there stopped.

"Never mind the key!"

"He ain't coming back," Randall said and showed a razor-thin smile; he spoke softly. "Your brother's gone, man."

"Carlos!"

No answer. Silence from the room. Carlos was gone and I was alone

"Just listen to Randall for a second," Marija said.

"Shut up," I said. I was holding a gun on two naked people yet I was the one losing authority by the second. Then it clicked: Carlos had the money. He had gone out a window.

I hadn't fired a gun since those camping days in the Minnesota woods. My arm muscles were stiffening up. The more time they had to keep conning us, the worse it was going to be for me. My torso was turned awkwardly because of the drag on my arm from the handcuff. I knew Randall was imagining his hands around one of the weapons he had stashed. Marija was thinking the same thing. It was just a question which one moved first and left the other one standing there to catch any bullets I might fire off in a panic.

I thought of that effeminate math teacher and wondered how he'd like knowing his words so long ago were prophetic. The chain was beneath the table top. It would be one shot, no more time because he would know his best time to make a move was before my brother returned, and the odds would change back in my favor. I tried to remember my father's advice: "Grip, stance, sight alignment, picture." Come on, Jack, picture it in your mind and put the bullet there – there, right there!

I featured the angle where the bullet had to go. Both of them stared at me. I leaned slightly so that the chain would go taut and hoped neither would trip to what I was going to do next.

I let my breath out slowly and soundlessly and waited for time to slow down to grains of moments and then microns. I twitched – something gave me away. Calderone moved at the same time I whipped my arm under the table. If he had been coming at me instead of sideways through the kitchen door, he'd have slammed my head into the table and that would have been that. Game over. I put the barrel up against the chain and fired off a round. I shattered wood and blew splinters into my hand from the blowback. I shot again and missed the entire chain.

Marija was on me by then. He body hit me hard enough to buckle my legs and crumple me to the floor but not hard enough to dislodge the gun. She flung her body over my back reaching for it – a mistake that enabled me to adjust my body. Her teeth sank into my shoulder while her fingers tore at my face to find my eyes. I had a clear view of the chain above me and I risked it all to shoot it and not her. If I failed, I was a dead man. She would climb my body and smother me with her weight in the confined space. The gun fired, my arm dropped like lead, and I dug the scalding barrel deep into her ribs. She howled and bucked.

I squeezed off another round where it would rip her heart into pulp but nothing happened. Either the gun jammed or the magazine was empty, but it was not a time to wonder. I pulled my arm back for some momentum before she could anticipate me and cracked her hard with the gun to the side of her face. It stunned her, but it didn't dislodge her because there wasn't enough force behind the blow. She whipped her arm out and hit my forearm at the exact place to cause the gun to drop. I grabbed a hank of her hair and tried to twist her head down. At the same time I tried to scoot out from beneath her, but she was slippery and strong. She was now on my midsection and primed for some real damage, and I had the terrifying fear that Calderone would come raging back into the room and squash me flat while she occupied me with her flailing claws.

She howled some animal gibberish at me and flung her hands at my face for another go at my eyes. I swung my fist toward the center of her face to split her hands like fighting a southpaw, and it worked. The wallop blinded her and smashed nose cartilage. I threw a right hand at her jaw and that toppled her over. She went sideways into the table edge and the blow knocked her out.

I scrambled out from beneath her and ran into the room where Carlos had gone. A rag of a curtain fluttered over a window. I went through it headfirst taking the thin curtain with me like a dirty shroud and landed in the overgrown grass and scrub brush that had grown up to the house. It was only a six-foot drop but it winded me.

Chunks of window frame and rotten board blew out

above me just as the ricochet of automatic gunfire. I lay there for a long second like a rabbit frozen in fear and then I started rolling. When my body and my mind came back together, I slung myself around and kept low and crawled. The slugs tore into the ground behind me but I was moving too fast as he raked the edges of the house's foundation in the belief I was still close. Calderone flew through the window and dropped to the ground. Then I heard random bursts from the gun and saw the muzzle flash as he raked the rifle back and forth in a scything motion. A flock of birds roosting in the tall grass near me exploded into the air. I lay still and listened. I heard a car starting up out front of the house.

Calderone heard it too. He cursed and sprayed a fusillade of hot lead in all directions.

I heard a car engine sputter-close.

Marija was out of the fight. That could only be my brother.

I heard the engine cough again and grind. He was flooding the engine in his panic. I fixed in my mind where the sound was coming from and imagined the road we had driven up. At the first bend before the house came into view was a cleared space that separated the orchards for the farm's tractors and wagons. It was too dark to see anything clearly. If I bolted, I could hit a tree and knock myself out. I could turn an ankle, but waiting to be hunted down was far worse. I ran headlong into brambles and pricker bushes which punctured me for invading their nocturnal space – twigs snapped as I bulled my way through the foliage. Branches lashed my eyes. I left my shirt in a patch of briars and kept running. I had that angle fixed like a satellite's coordinates in my brain. Pre-dawn light was breaking through the trees in the direction of my running. I saw a misty flame of fog rise from the marshes. I burst through a ditch where loose strife grew in bunches and almost lost my shoes in the muddy soil.

I heard another volley from the assault rifle. Another car coming fast – it was slewing from one side of the road to the other and the engine whined in low gear.

I broke through the brush where he'd have to slow to negotiate the last bend before the gravel road straightened out. He was coming too fast.

The car careened toward me, and I leaped out of the way before it rumbled into a steep drainage ditch.

Carlos, you bastard, stop! But Carlos wasn't stopping.

I saw the mud kicked up from its spinning tires and picked myself up from the dirt. The ditch was soft earth but not steep enough to stop the car from forward progress. Once he had it back on the road surface, he'd be gone, and I'd be the quarry again.

The car bounced on its chassis as he brought it up and hit the gas hard. Pebbles spun around in the wheel well and missed me by inches. I gave it everything I had left. I held nothing back when I dove for the driver's side door. If I missed, I'd never have the strength to pick myself up.

My hand cupped the latch and it popped open enough for Carlos to turn his head and see me sprawled in the ditch.

"I thought you were dead," he said with a lopsided grin.

I lifted my head and started crawling toward him. He jammed the car in park and got out; he helped me to my feet and guided me into the back seat.

"Jesus fuck Christ, Jack, what the fuckin' fuck!"

I pressed my face against the car seat. "Tired, can't run anymore."

He let out a cowboy whoop as he slung us onto 531 with the car bucking so hard on the rough shoulders I heard a wheel cover come loose. He floored it on the open road. The first thing I was aware of was the familiar pungent odor. I opened my eyes and saw the duffel bag lying on the floorboard. Packets of money and loose bills lay all around. The back draft of the speeding car sent tiny flutters among twenty-dollar bills swirling up in a vortex like slats of a roof caught in a twister.

When I was able to sit upright, I said, "What happened to that key you were looking for?"

He flashed me a huge smile from up front. He had a gold molar I'd never noticed before. His eyes were glassy again and the sweat dripped from his neck into the collar of his shirt.

"Let's say we're even, bro," he said.

"I can live with that," I said.

Flying through the dark of back country roads, a smile lit my face. I saw Carlos glance into the rearview mirror. "What's funny, Jack?"

"I'm alive," I said. "You remember that math teacher, what's-his-name?"

"Devereux," Carlos said. "Old man Devereux, yes."

"He used to say the Pythagorean theorem would save our lives one day."

When Carlos turned around, I was crying, shedding big tears, and then I was sobbing like a baby. My brother did me the kindness of turning around and not speaking for the next hour.

#26

He drove east into the sun staying on the country roads. The magenta sky became ochre and then a washed-out blue. The gold-fringed cumulo-nimbus clouds were the loveliest sight my battered eyes had ever seen. I was not being dissected, I was not being beaten with fists or feet, I was not being flayed or fricasseed or sautéed. Jack had climbed down the beanstalk.

"Where the fucking fuck we at?" he asked me. The sun was just clearing the tree line. I rolled down the windows to wash out some of the car's reek. My clothes were dank, my body odoriferous, and my legs and feet soaked and full of seed pods and briars. Nature was oblivious to motivations.

"Denmark," I said.

He nodded as if that made sense and kept driving. We passed through the center of town, a dismal square of shut-up shops and glazed windows where placards announced sales of farms.

"Jesus love a duck, fucking Christ," Carlos said and pointed at a black buggy through the windshield. "They got those whatchamacallems here, Amish."

"Go north, you'll hit the Route Ninety junction. Connects Seattle to New York City." I said. "Take your pick, Carlos."

"You're coming with me, man."

"No," I said. "I'm going back."

"You're on the run like me now, nigga. Cops or Calderone, shit, I don't know which is worse. But I know you ain't got a woman or a home to go back to."

As he slowed just enough for the final stop sign leading out of town, I hopped out and covered the driver's side window with my body. There was nothing but an identical bleak county ahead just like the ones we had passed through. He squinted up at me through the rays of sun streaming in.

"Hey, what the fuck's this? You've got to come with me."

"I liked what I had before you showed up."

"You're crazy, man."

"I came by it honestly," I said.

"I got mine the hard way," he said. "I just can't stay within the lines no more, Jack."

"We all make choices, brother," I said. I stretched my

back again. It burned like ice where she had bit me.

"No catching up then, eh?" he said. What would have been the point, I wondered; most of our choices were made for us a long time ago. I didn't say anything but he seemed resigned to it. I knew he'd think me left behind wouldn't make a bad red herring and it was like something the old man used to quote from his Stalin period: "Two can keep a secret if one is dead."

We shook hands like brothers, though, through the open window, and I watched him drive off. About twenty yards ahead, he hit the brakes hard and my heart stopped. I knew he had a gun. When he was about five yards from me, I was prepared to bolt, but then I saw a packet of money come flying out the window in a high arc and land in front of me.

Fifties. They didn't smell too bad, no worse than I did anyway, standing at the edge of a sleepy town square on a morning in early September. The undersides of tree leaves had a dull color like pewter that shimmered to silver when the breeze lifted them up. The whole square smelled of dust and manure.

I picked up the bag behind me and started to walk back the way we came. I never heard the tires squeal or the ear-splitting scream, but I could imagine them easily enough.

Forty yards in the distance was a fallow field, and I headed at a trot diagonally across it. At the edge of the field about three acres distant was a ravine where I could lie until sundown.

My brother wouldn't risk hanging around long – not with Calderone and a dead body behind him and all the cops in the state converging on these roads. He might be stoned enough to ask a few locals if they'd seen a stranger carrying a bag, but sooner or later the looks they'd give him would tell him to flee or risk capture.

I meant to find a café around supper time and then sit and have coffee until I spotted some bored farm kid with a car and no money who wouldn't ask questions about someone who kept a hand in his pocket to hide a dangling cuff link. I'd offer him a couple of the fifties my brother had gifted me – a little *lagniappe* as the French Canucks used to say in Montreal. I imagined that good deed had him standing in a black rage in front of his own ass-kicking machine wherever he was as he replayed how I must have scuttled out the door with the bag at my feet. Find the weakness, Carlos, I said to the opalescent sky high above the ditch, playing my father.

It turned out to be the dishwasher in the café who was my ride home. He got off at nine-thirty so I had to kill some time back in my ditch. His name was George and he asked me if I wanted anything else from him. I thanked him and said the ride would be sufficient. I told him a long, sad story about coming home and finding my wife run off with a boyfriend and the cops called on me for decking her when she came back for the TV. It was plausible and close enough to the truth.

I told him to drop me off at Point Park at the end of my street. No lights were on in the house and no cars sat out front. He said if I was locked out, he'd go halfers on a motel with me if I changed my mind. I declined and said no, I wasn't locked out, although that part of my story wasn't true. It wasn't mine now and nothing else there was mine except some tools in the garage, a big rain barrel, and the lingering smell of a corpse's recent occupancy.

Calderone left death and horror in his wake like the Four Horsemen. But I knew deep in the cockles of my own rotten heart that we make our own sorrows.

THURSDAY, SEPTEMBER 9

6:15 A.M.

#27

Pippin found me the next morning at sunup sitting on my front steps, which I was now calling my ex-front steps to my ex-house owned by my almost ex-wife. He slammed on the brakes of his Navigator and was out of the car and striding up the slope of my ex-grass.

"You want to explain yourself?" he said.

"I don't know what you're referring to, Agent Pippin."

"I'm referring to a dead body back there!" he shouted. "A dead woman! Lying choked to death on some shitty couch in some crappy farmhouse!" His arm waved behind him and his finger poked holes in the air for emphasis. "There! Back there! Twenty fucking miles from where you're sitting with a goddamned smirk on your face!"

"That's not a smirk," I said. "It's a rictus grin."

"Don't play games with me, God damn you!"

For a long second he looked at me with raw hatred seeping from his eyes, and I thought he was going to lunge for my throat.

"Where have you been?" This, much calmer, the SAC in command again.

"I've been around," I said. "Here and there."

His eyes reversed direction: from slits to popped; a worm-like vein of blood was ticking along his right temple.

"OK, so that's how you want to play it," he said. He pulled out a cell phone and spoke into it. The conversation was truncated down to syllables but all the pronoun references were pointing to me.

"Am I under arrest?"

Pippin stared at me. His wrath softened a fraction. "What has happened to you, man?"

"What do you mean?"

"You look like death eating a sandwich." He stared at me hard.

"Summer colds are the worst," I said.

"Summer cold, my shiny buffed black ass. Colds don't swell up your face like that. They don't turn you black and blue and make your eyes look like piss holes in a snowbank. You got the slim disease, Jack? You're twenty pounds lighter since the last time I saw you."

"The portrait in my attic must be aging," I said.

"What the fuck are you sayin'?"

"Never mind," I said.

"For a gardener that never got a high-school diploma,

you got a lot of smart-assed things to say," Pippin shot back.

"Landscaper," I said making long syllables out of it.

"OK, land-sca-per. Take a ride with me. I want to show you something," he said.

"I need to shower first," I said. "I smell bad."

"Yeah, I picked that up when I was downwind, but it seemed a minor point to bring to your attention given the rest of your new look."

"She put a new door in," I said. "I can't get inside."

"Jesus Christ, you idiot, go ask a neighbor if you can use the shower. Stop wasting my motherfucking time here, man!"

Only one of my neighbors would come to the door. She told me her plumbing was broken. I didn't blame them. I tried Paul's bed-and-breakfast across the street but no one there would acknowledge my knock. Sarah would be pitied as much as I was being reviled for the chaos I had brought to this quiet street in this small town.

Pippin drove me to the Salvation Army where I cashed another fifty in for some shirts, pants and shoes, and a gym bag. He took me to a motel on the freeway where I showered while he sat on the bed and made several phone calls, one all the way to DC headquarters.

"I'm sorry to take you out of your way," I said rubbing myself down with a thick cotton towel. Hot water had never felt so good. I had gorged on bags of potato chips and candy bars from the vending machine in the lobby. I went back to toweling my hair.

"Whoah, Nellie. You look like somebody held you by the feet and ran you through a meat grinder. What happened to your neck? Are those bite marks?"

"Date last night."

"Uh-huh, like those ligature marks on your wrist?"

"I dig rough sex," I said.

"This isn't my first rodeo, shithead. We're gonna have us a long talk about your hobbies."

"That bed looks good. Would you mind if I took a brief catnap, Agent Pippin? Just ten minutes. I feel as if I haven't slept in three days."

"Get in the goddamned car," he said.

#28

He turned down the driveway and parked behind an ambulance with the driver giving him a bored salute. On the porch, I saw a detective talking to some people in jackets with the ERT logo on the back. One of them carried a trajectory rod in his hand.

"We're still making casts of the tire tracks," Pippin said. "Walk behind me."

At the back of the ambulance, he paused. "The M.E. took an hour to get here. I had my own forensics people up here by then. If I ever decide to become a serial killer and dump bodies, I'm coming to this county."

His stride was long. He stopped and turned around.

"The place was stripped clean. People left in a hurry but they forgot to take something with them." He opened the doors of the ambulance and climbed in. A black body bag was strapped onto a gurney.

He offered me a hand. "Come on up," he said.

I climbed in and he led me to the back of the ambulance. He unzipped the body bag down to her pubis. Half her face was missing. The lone eyeball that was intact stared straight up behind her.

"Seen her before?"

"You know I have, Pippin," I said.

"They probably used a fragmentation slug, do that kind of damage. Why strangle her? See the hand marks around her neck?"

"Her name is Tanya. I don't know much else about her," I said.

"We're going to superglue her for prints," he said. "But that'll lead to dick. Help me here, Jack." My mind replayed Calderone's big hand wrapped around her neck pressing her into the back of the sofa while he slammed into her. Did she know what was happening?

"They find the gun?"

"We're still looking," Pippin said. "I've got some metal detectors coming up. We're using the sheriff's people to sweep around the house."

"I'm not her kin," I said. "I can't legally identify her."

"I thought you might want to see what you and your skinhead brothers-"

"Randall Calderone's not my brother," I said.

His height made it hard for him to move around inside the ambulance, but he had me by the arms, and I was surprised by his anger. His eyes were bloodshot. I wasn't the only one going without sleep. He shoved me backward out of the ambulance so fast that I hit the dirt and went down on one knee.

"You want to remember you've got people from the house looking at us," I said.

I managed to get to my feet and was brushing off the road grit from my second-hand clothes when he threw me against the side of the ambulance.

"You creepy son of a bitch! You have ice for blood? I showed you what your friend and his cellmate, your own flesh-and-blood brother did to that little girl back there."

"I can't help you, Agent Pippin."

"Can't or won't? You know what happened to her, and I want to know what you know!"

His ring tones went off. I recognized the opening notes of a song made popular by England's blue-eyed soul singer, Lisa Stansfield. Sarah had all her CDs. Pippin spoke a few clipped words, snapped his cell shut and slipped it back into his belt.

He looked at me. "It's foolish to be worried about you. You're a cold fish, Jack." He told me to stay put and walked away. I looked over at the ambulance driver who stared back at me with loathing and curiosity.

Pippin left me there for an hour while he was inside. The ride back to the motel was made in grim silence with Pippin staring straight ahead. For whatever reason, he decided to break the silence with an odd comment: "One of our guys dug up some Interpol info on Calderone's woman. She's related to Ante Pavelić."

"Who's he when he's at home?"

"She didn't mention that in her pillow talk, huh? She's related to a big shot. He was the head of the wartime quisling regime in Croatia," Pippin said.

"I'll bet a person doesn't get more than one or two chances in life to use a word like that," I said. What was wrong with me anyhow? I wondered. The man could have had me cuffed in a cramped interrogation room, and all I seemed to do was goad him.

When he dropped me off at my motel, he said, "I've got a first-class polygrapher coming up today. I want him to test you."

"Be glad to oblige, Agent Pippin," I said and tried out a brief smile.

He looked at me with pure disgust. "It's no wonder your wife left you," he said.

#29

I knew that when they found the gun it would have my prints all over it. Marija's idea, probably. Calderone's style was more like writing my name in block letters on the bathroom mirror with a bar of soap. I wasn't in the databases used by US law enforcement, but my prints were taken by the Coast Guard in Cleveland when I applied for my seaman's ticket years ago. Canada was stringent about sealing juvie records. My father had done everything he knew to make us invisible to the government's reach, but nobody's good enough to do that for long. All Pippin had to do to match the prints he'd find on the gun would be to throw a little carbon dust on my side of the car or any door handle upstairs in my room.

I hit my bed with my clothes and shoes still on. I slept until 4:05 when the phone became an intolerable wail. "I'm coming down," I said and hung up.

Pippin wore a different suit. He looked like one of Northtown's local yachties, one of the doctors, lawyers or stockbrokers who comprised the upper class and swapped wives among their own kind. Pippin's blue blazer and gray slacks with their razor creases down the front complemented an off-white shirt and silver tie that looked as if it had been dipped in Day-Glo paint. It flashed with different geometric shapes.

"You look spiffy," I said.

"What kind of word is that?"

"It means nice," I said.

"Then say 'nice,' damn it," he said. "I've been waiting down here in this heat."

That seemed odd considering he kept the a/c in the car at morgue temperature.

His Navigator hadn't been washed to disguise any telltale marks where my prints might have been lifted from the finish. I was getting as paranoid as the old man in his latter days.

"We're going to use the local sheriff's," he said. "It's in Jefferson about six miles from here."

"I live here, Forzell," I said. "I've been all the way to Youngstown once."

I managed to get a few facts from him but nothing that wouldn't be splashed all over the front pages of the paper tomorrow morning. Her larynx was crushed, petechial hemorrhaging in the lone white of the eyeball meant strangulation occurred prior to the gunshot that left a snowstorm in her brain and would have turned her eyeball black.

"The head shot wasn't necessary," Pippin said. "Why do you suppose that is?"

"Coup de theâtre," I said.

"Did your momma make you swallow a dictionary when you was a kid?"

"No, my father," I said. "Maybe it was done to disguise the forensics."

"You been watchin' too many assheaded forensics shows on TV with all that computer-generated nonsense."

"Did you find the gun?"

"We found guns," he said. "Whole bunch of them, in fact. Ballistics doesn't work on fragments, in case you were worried, but I hear we've got some good thirteen-point prints on a couple of them. We're running them through AFIS and NCIC."

He turned off the Jefferson exit and started to turn left.

"Go right. It's the other way," I said.

"Why not put a damned sign up? You know, with an arrow, maybe? Is this some kind of hillbilly thing up here?"

"You're not getting much sleep yourself, are you, Agent Pippin?"

He let that go. "You know who Youngstown's most famous crook was, Jack?"

"Yeah, he just died. A tractor fell on him, I heard," I said.

"No, not him. Not even close. Emil Denzio. Youngstown bank robber, a legend back in the sixties and seventies."

"Why does he have to do with me?"

"Emil was a real smart guy. Like you. But you know how he and his crew fucked up?"

"They bragged," I said.

"Not a bad guess, but no. They did their biggest score in Las Vegas. He knew everybody would figure it for a Denzio job, so he had his boys clean up the house where they were planning their score, scrubbed it from top to bottom. But they forgot to check the dish washer. Can you believe it? Everybody's prints all over the dishes. Bagged them all in a week – phhht, like that." He tossed an imaginary jail key out the window.

"Too bad he wasn't mobbed up," I said.

"Huh, why's that?"

"Because Hoover was running the bureau then. The Chicago mob blackmailed him with photos of him and Clive Tolson, the number-two man at the FBI."

"Jack, that's old shit, and nobody cares Hoover was a homo or a drag queen or whatever the fuck," he said.

"He was a transvestite," I said. "They used to call him J. Edna behind his back. You don't know your bureau mythology, Pippin."

"There you go again. Just when I think we got us a little rapport goin' on, you have to go and say something like that." He shook his head at me, an errant pupil who missed the lesson in the parable. Except that I hadn't: fingerprints. Mine. He intended to nail me on them.

We parked behind the court house and walked to the sheriff's office in the adjacent building. He introduced me to the polygrapher and said he would wait for me downstairs.

"How soon will I have the results?" I asked.

He just stared at me and trotted out his best blaccent for the reply: "Ya'll know when you're tellin' a fib, don't you?"

I was in the room for forty-seven minutes before the polygrapher came in. He had that faraway, worried look some professionals get. He sniffed like a prairie dog and mumbled his name but didn't offer to shake my hand. When it was over, he folded the sheets and left me sitting there with the blood-pressure cuff still attached. Pippin strode into the room as if on cue and undid my cuff. "Let's go."

When we were outside, he said, "You mind if I axe you somethin'?"

"You can drop the ghettospeak, Forzell. I know that you were Phi Beta Kappa and Columbia Law wasn't filling a racial quota when they admitted you."

"How did-"

"Hillbilly towns have libraries and computers too," I said and got out of the car in the back of the lot.

I was starving. The overpass exchange was a hub of fast-food franchises, which was like Tantalus' situation. I wanted to walk down the aisle of a supermarket and see real food. The night air was cold enough to raise gooseflesh on my arms.

"My man said he's never seen anything like that reading. You made a casserole out of the test questions and the base questions both. How did you do it? Some convict trick, right, like drinking a couple Coca-Colas, swallow some aspirin, maybe?"

I stretched and heard vertebrae crack all the way down my spine. "I answered the questions," I said.

"I promised myself I wasn't going to lose my temper with you again," he said. "I'll see you tomorrow."

"Maybe some people control their emotions better," I said.

"You mean, like some woodpeckers get headaches and some don't?"

I watched him drive off. I saw the stars overhead. The autumn sky was shifting the constellations into the new tangents and angles of the autumnal rotation in sidereal time. The headlights ahead disappeared in the traffic.

"It's like this," I said to the empty elevator. "You take one rogue, insane CIA agent and you turn him loose on a couple boys. Then you count the ways he can fuck with their minds."

From my tiny balcony, I gazed at the night sky wheeling overhead as it had for millennia and would until our second-rate star collapsed in on itself, all fuel spent. Sodium lights and smog from the plastics factories and power plants near the shoreline obscured everything but the brightest of stars and turned part of the horizon orange. High up, just beneath Polaris, Altair, Deneb and Vega reformed their isosceles triangle. The sizzling din of traffic below the overpass on Interstate 90 took my thoughts away from the stars back down to this planet, this flyspeck rock in a vast, dark universe of emptiness and cold.

I wondered how far my brother had motored since that morning. I wondered how long I was going to last this time without somebody else putting some kind of cuff on me. Stamina – wasn't that Marija's word?

#30

"I want to see you," she said. "I'm downstairs in the lobby."

I didn't recognize the voice right away. I told her I'd be right down. I checked the time: ten oh-seven. I had sated my ravenous hunger with more bags of greasy snack food and felt the clot in my protesting stomach.

Alicia Fox-Whitcomb wasn't dressed for work either. She wore a beige pants suit with a casual look that belied her curves. The pendulum of my sexualized mind put her in the middle with Sarah in her faded Levi's at one end and Marija – wanton, sans clothes, and brazen in her sexuality – at the other.

There was something I liked about the woman the first

time I saw her – the regal walk, maybe, something indefinable; she wasn't attractive or fine-boned or even aging gracefully for that matter. Words like 'class' and 'grace' seemed too remote.

She cut me a quick smile when I exited the lobby elevator and then, as before, it disappeared and remade itself into a bland corporate stare.

"We can have coffee and talk here," I said. The motel offered a miniature comfort room, or whatever their brochures called a nook where you could eat a stale donut and drink their watery coffee. I took a rubbery Danish from the tray and set it back down.

She glanced around the room and dismissed it. "Let's walk outside," she said.

The sun was high and the air had that fall tang without letting go of summer, the between-times feeling that life gives you sometimes when you remember all the promises you failed to keep.

"I'm leaving," she said.

"Ohio or your job?"

"Both, everything," she said. "My family, too."

"I see," I said. I didn't. I expected this to be payback, an overdue delivery on a promissory note when she spat in my face. She was here to point me out and Pippin would leap from behind the next hedge with a pair of shiny handcuffs.

We were close to the overpass exit where the traffic below was starting to affect the decibel level of our conversation. Crows in some poplar trees on the Austinburgh side of the freeway communicated in their cree-caw dialect above the din. Why was it called a murder of crows? My unfocused mind drifted with a dull fascination at everything and nothing. I was blitzing too many brain cells with beatings and booze. And mostly I was enervated from the sheer tension of waiting for more violence to seek me out. Sarah's grandmother had died in the rehab center out here; we used to bring her favorite Finnish casseroles. Captain John Brown, with his flaming red beard, struggled on a homestead not far from here before his abolitionist obsession told him to stockpile weapons in his barn for the coming slaughter.

"We're going away together," Alicia said.

I knew she didn't mean her husband by that. Once again, I pictured the woman scolding and cursing me from Danko's driveway.

"We're in love," she said. "We've been in love for years," she said. A wisp of hair blew across her forehead. She gave off a lavender scent that seemed right for the time and the place.

"Love," I repeated. I didn't know what else to say.

"You haven't asked me why I haven't identified you," she said. "That's the one question anyone in your situation should want to know first."

"Would you feel any better if I said it kept me up at night?"

"No, not really, Mister Trichaud."

"I think, after all that's happened, we should be on a first-name basis by now."

"You're an odd man, Jack."

"People keep saying that. They're probably right."

I had not said a word to her inside her house on that awful day. I wasn't going to insult her by saying I was sorry.

"I met her on the internet three years ago. I can't live without her. She loves me too."

"Have you-"

"Have I told my family? Yes – and no. We've been planning to tell our families this for a long time... and then – and then Phil, that's Emma's husband, when he got called up for that thing in Afghanistan, and then you three showed up and threatened to ruin us by revealing our... secret."

"I know," I said.

"Nothing's gone right since that day. It's as if I – none of us – can move on with our lives."

The traffic was a softer roar below us. "I've given two weeks' notice at work. We're leaving for California at the end of the month."

I nodded. Why make this revelation – confession? – to me, I wondered.

Maybe my expression made her laugh, but it was a bitter laugh. "I don't know why I'm telling you this before I've told Brandi or David."

She faced me directly.

"Why haven't you turned me in?" I asked. "There's an FBI agent who's playing cat-and-mouse with me, but that's going to end soon," I said.

"Will you be going to prison?"

"I assume so. They take a dim view of kidnapping and armed robbery in this state."

How had my fool of a brother ever thought this woman was the kind who fell for the Stockholm syndrome?

She brushed hair out of her face. I noticed her wedding

band was off. "That FBI agent. He even calls me at work about you."

"I was part of what put you and your family through a nightmare that no one should have to experience," I said.

"Will it help if I say I won't forgive you?"

"Maybe."

"I notice you haven't formally said you're sorry for it."

I stopped and looked down at the two lanes, the filthy tops of semis whistling past, and wished I was joining them.

"Because you saved Brandi," she said.

"I don't understand."

"My husband told me about it."

I remembered looking once into her husband's face and seeing his eyes pleading with me, but that was just a flicker and it was gone.

"The agent told me about this Randall Calderone. He said we were lucky to get out alive, all of us."

"I won't disagree with that," I said.

Pippin told me that the next time Calderone saw a judge he'd get one of those Buck Rogers sentences where he'd be released in the twenty-fifth century if they didn't stick him with a lethal injection, which is the more likely.

"He – David – said that Calderone was going to take Brandi upstairs. He said he looked into that bastard's face and he knew what he was going to do."

Carlos was too stoned to even notice what was going to happen.

"You stopped him, you stopped him…"

Then she cried, and I held her in my arms and tried to tell her I was so sorry, so very sorry. She sobbed in my arms like a mother, not a businesswoman or a wife. Just a mother whose child had experienced a terrible ordeal and come so close to a much worse one.

"I'm sorry, too," she said and smeared tears and makeup with the back of her hand. She took some kleenex out of her purse and wiped her face clear of everything. "I had Brandi late in life. That doesn't matter, does it? No one is prepared for it," she said.

"No," I agreed. None of us is prepared for any of it.

I remembered Calderone's face close to mine, my hand grasping his wrist with the knife. He gave me that convict grin, flipped me the bird, and retreated back to the den, where he stayed until morning. I didn't think Brandi or her father were aware of any of it.

"About the money-" I began.

"I'm not interested in the money," she said. "We're insured. Besides, the bank's portfolio is over four billion annually."

"So what happens now?"

"Once I've told my family and made arrangements with David, I'm never coming back here. I'm not wasting any more years of my life being unhappy. Brandi's a young woman now. She'll have to cope with... with this new arrangement," Alicia said.

It was a conversation between a man and a woman overlooking a freeway overpass. No one observing would ever guess what mayhem lay beneath it.

She seemed to recover some of her steel. "Do you believe in God?"

"My father used to quote Shakespeare," I said. "'As flies are to wanton boys we are to the gods. They kill us for their sport.'" Pippin had asked me that, too. Odd.

"Maybe we weren't the best Catholics. David and I were making a good life, we had Brandi to think of, our careers. The money was good. It makes you..."

She paused. I waited for her to find the words for it, whatever it was.

"It makes you forget," she said finally, happy with the choice. "It's like being awake and asleep at the same time. But time passes, you grow older. Unfortunately, not always wiser."

She gave me another quick smile but it wasn't like the practiced one; it was more a throwback to one she might have used before her professional career taught her to hide emotion, lower her voice to a man's pitch.

"I know something about forgetting," I said. "My wife, that is, my ex-wife, said I was very good at it."

"My husband reads the bible. Maybe it's overcompensation for what he has to do on his job, but he's a very good, kind man. He gave me this for you. Read it later, please."

She handed me a slip of paper and turned around and started walking back. I watched her for a while and then I cut across a field behind Burger King to the rear of my motel.

The semis passed close enough to give me the acrid whiff of heated diesel fuel. The meadow was full of Queen-Ann's-Lace and Monarchs delaying their trip to Mexico for the abundance of flowers. The newspaper said honey bees were all dying of a hive disorder; the monarch butterflies were being killed off by pollution.

Most of the poplars that survived the state's periodic

road widening efforts were stunted from the blunt force of sleety winter winds banging into them. They weren't as striking to the eye as the firs and spruce that made a phalanx at the edges of the snow fences but there were many kinds in one section. Someone a long time ago must have loved that tree. I saw some blacks near a balsam, a few gray and, for this northern climate, the rare Lombardy. Near it a small stand of swamp cottonwoods and some silver and yellow poplars grew wild.

Maybe I was mistaken from the distance, but it looked to me as if that old farmer, whoever he was, had planted a single Balm-of-Gilead in their midst. Before I had gone ten feet, my Salvation Army shoes were soaked. My pant legs were sodden and dusted with pollen. I had an urge to make a bouquet of the painted trillium. The white clusters beside the ditches at the bottom of the ravine were all in bloom: Lizard's Tail, Canada Mayflower, and False Solomon's Seal. I always liked weeds.

Up in my room I thought about Alicia. The old man's ghost, however, was nodding in approval at me because I had beaten the polygraph.

I opened the folded paper and read:

> Then the young man answered, 'I have heard, Brother Azarias, that this maid hath been given to seven men, who all died in the marriage chamber.' Because that she had been married to seven husbands, whom Asmodeus the evil spirit had killed before they had lain with her.
> – Book of Tobit

I had gone through a phase of religious reading during one of my seasons on the Great Lakes as a deckhand, but the passage mystified me. Brandi was the maid and Calderone clearly usurped the demon's role, but was I Brother Azarias or Raphael in disguise? The only thing I ever had in common with an archangel was the fact that I was sent on missions by a much stronger force, far greater in power than mine and downright malevolent when disobeyed.

#31

I found a slip of paper under my door when I got back. The handwriting was feminine with childish whorls and loops, although the message wasn't. It was written in pencil, unsigned, on the back of a packing slip sent to the motel:

> Your brother for the money

There was also a telephone message from Rick saying I should thank Augie for talking him out of filing criminal charges against me. He cursed me out, but that was being stoned with popcorn. The Big Crapshooter Who Rules the Board must have found it amusing to extricate me from one dangerous enterprise while dipping me headfirst into another. I didn't understand Marija's note – who else? – because my brother should have been in New York City by nightfall yesterday. Was Pippin fishing with me as bait?

I sat down on the bed and rubbed my temples and tried to think. I wanted another tête-à-tête with Randall Calderone about as much as I wanted a hot lead enema. My shoulder burned where Marija's teeth marks had raised the flesh into an oozing circular welt. Nothing dirtier than a human mouth, and I made a mental note to get a tetanus before it turned septic.

I had enough money stashed in my sneakers to put all this behind me. I could leave scot-free, get on a Greyhound, pick a new spot on the map. I had gone soft during those nine years of marriage and lost my edge. The trouble was, much as I hated to admit it, I liked being another Northtown drone, an ordinary, tax-paying nobody.

But every time I told myself Carlos was long gone, that infallible dread in the pit of my stomach told me the opposite. The whole premise he wouldn't run for cover was so stupid and incredible – and that's what made it believable.

It was time for me to stop playing the tethered goat waiting to get eaten by the wolf. I left a message for Pippin and asked him to call me back.

Five minutes later, he called. I picked up on the first ring and put a husky dip in my voice. "Agent Pippin, you're like a lot of intelligent people I've met in my travels. You're intensely stupid."

"Whoa, slow down, Trichaud. What are you talking about?"

"You won't catch Calderone by watching me twenty-four, seven," I said.

"Who says I'm watching you?"

"If I flipped this curtain, would I see the one guy in the Blazer, and the other one who followed us this morning, the one in the tan Datsun behind Burger King? I noticed a home decorating van in the lot. I suppose that's you."

"What do you want, Trichaud?"

"You're not thinking like him and if you're going to find him, you have to try to do that."

"And you know how to do that?"

"He thinks in capital letters."

"Explain."

"I received a note this morning."

"God damn it, I'm coming up."

#32

"It's open," I said.

He came in as dapper and nattily dressed as ever despite being on a stakeout. I wondered how much luggage he traveled with.

"Was Alicia your idea?"

"What do you think, Jack?"

"Was she wired?"

He looked at me and shrugged. "She wouldn't allow it," he said. "I don't know what evil spell you've cast on that woman-"

"Did you get anything? I mean from a guy with a long-range mic or anything?"

"You mean anything I can use in court? You already know the answer to that one. That's why you stood in the middle of that overpass, isn't it? Our guy in Burger King was zeroed on your mug but he said the traffic noise was deafening."

"So how did Marija get under my door with all your surveillance?"

"She didn't. You have any idea how many neo-Nazi organizations are holed up in this raggedy-assed state?"

"Calderone is Aryan Brotherhood," I said. "I thought their ideology went into their tattoos and the rest was extortion and being a silent partner in running prisons for the US government."

"They might not be big on reading Nietzsche during long winter nights but they work with anybody, and they're not just prisons," Pippin said. "Get to the point, Jack."

"Read this," I said and handed him the note.

Pippin eyeballed my room. "Could have been a maid whose old man is locked up and somebody put the arm on him so he calls her and tells her to pick up the note at point A and slip it under your door."

"So he just looked into his little black book and found a name who owned a deserted farm house?"

"I don't know what you mean, Jack."

"But that's how he got the guns," I said.

"DEA's looking into it. They're tracing them now."

"You don't know much, do you, Pippin?"

"We'll check the motel surveillance tape, OK? The cameras don't pan so we don't see far from the elevators. You think some greasy-looking biker with a swastika on his forehead is going to come walking right up to your door?"

"Let me help you," I said.

"I don't work with criminals, I put them in jail."

He slammed the door and took the note with him. He never asked me what it meant. I was the one underestimating him.

#33

I called Stevie's cab company but didn't ask for her. When a car with the same livery showed up outside the lobby and gave a triple honk I walked nonchalantly to it and smiled for all the CCTV lenses. My heart was racing and my esophagus burned from acid reflux. I awoke from a nap that had left me feeling sticky and tense. Alicia's words still haunted me.

I threw the bag in and asked him, "Is Stevie working now?"

"Naw," he said. "Stupid bitch came into some money and got her ass all wasted. Didn't show up for her shift two days straight. They canned her."

"That's too bad," I said.

"Said she found it in a dumpster, haw," he snorted. "Can you believe that shit? The fat dyke. So where we goin', buddy?"

I told the driver to take me into town but to take the first exit from the interstate north where I had him wait for me in front of the DYI. I threw my purchases inside and climbed in.

He drove fast without my prompting. Beside us the Northtown River flowed along in swirls before it flattened out into the brown chemical murk that eddied back and forth between the mouth of the lake and the docks of the marinas. My bespectacled driver happily informed me he was addicted to internet pornography and had married a Filipina mail-order bride from one of his web sites.

I had a gut-churning fear that, at the end of all this, no matter what I did to avoid it, I was going to confront a really vicious dog guarding the mouth of hell. Calderone didn't have three heads, but he used the two he had with a violence and fearlessness I had witnessed too often.

The cabbie let me off in front of the house. Sarah and her new beau were standing on the porch with grocery bags in their hands; she fiddled one-handedly with the key. As I approached the steps, she turned around to see me. The words she formed were like an exaggeration of an opera singer's pear-shaped notes: Oh shit.

"Jack, I don't want any trouble," she said.

"Hello, Sarah," I said.

I pressed the small device into her hand while her boyfriend concentrated on the bag in my other hand as if I were about to pull an Uzi out of it. She looked at me intensely but didn't betray me. I saw her close her hand around it.

I said, "I need a few tools from the garage, Sarah."

"There's a new lock on it," she said.

"Not a problem," I said and drew a crowbar out of the bag.

"Let him in with the key, hon," she said.

Then she muttered something under her breath about my timing and something else I didn't catch, but I inferred she wanted him to keep an eye on me. In less than two weeks, I had gone from total obscurity to being one of the most watched men in Northeastern Ohio. The Greeks were fond of irony but I was eating it for breakfast, lunch, and dinner.

As soon as she was inside the house, I said, "My name's Jack," and proffered my hand. He came down the steps, an owner's shuffle that matched the sneer on his face.

"Fuck you," he said.

I walked behind him up the driveway. An effort had been made to clean up some of the damage to the flower gardens.

He undid the lock and stepped aside. "Take what you need and get out."

I walked in and smelled that familiar odor of death. I went to the rain barrel with the tool handles jutting out like giant toothpicks from a black mouth. I reached in and pulled out the duffel bag. It felt like the right weight.

"I saw your punching bag in the basement," he said.

"Keep it," I said. "I'm first among equals when it comes to hitting a bag that didn't hit back."

"Next time you come around here without my

permission, I'll show you something that does hit back," he said.

"Thanks, I'll be sure to ask permission."

He wasn't even a tiny blip on my screen so it was something of a surprise to realize he loathed me enough to want to pick a fight with me. My mind was keyed to an airbus named Calderone; Sarah's new man was one of those balsa-wood gliders I used to buy with a quarter. Sarah was standing out front waiting for me.

Before I walked away, I thought I saw a look of concern on her face. "You look terrible, Jack," she said. I kept walking down the sidewalk, a pair of heavy bags looped over each shoulder.

I walked down to the beach and found a payphone near the concession stand the vandals hadn't wrecked yet. Since they all had cell phones anyway, that kind of mischief lost some of its appeal. Their preferred means of annoying the bourgeoisie escalated to garage thefts, spray painting houses, and tipping over memorials to fallen soldiers.

I dialed the number Stevie gave me, and waited while it went through a dozen rings. No answer. I hung up.

The jungle gym for the little kids was deserted. The wooden walkway extending from the tawny brick concession stand to the shoreline was empty of people. Far off near the shore on the private side, I saw a man walking a pair of German shepherds. The city workers hadn't gotten round to rolling up the beach for the winter season. It was too soon after Labor Day, and the water would still be around seventy degrees.

I had a crazy urge to run down the boardwalk and dive headfirst into the breakers. Let the waves roll me around and toss me wherever they wanted.

I dialed the number again and this time I heard her scratchy smoker's voice ask, "Who is it?"

"It's me," I said.

"Like, who the fuck's you?"

"The guy that owes you a lot of money," I said. "The same one that wants to give you more money for a few days of driving."

"Where youse at, Jack?"

I told her. She said she'd meet me in twenty minutes. I told her the name of a fish restaurant near the beach where Sarah always ordered the yellow perch.

"Give me a half hour," I said. "There's something I have to do first."

After secreting the bag back into its tidy fissure in the breakwall, I walked back up the hill, sweating hard now, and my shoulder bloody and raw from the constant rubbing. If they were ringing the phone off the hook back at the motel, it could work against Carlos – if they even had him. I had the money and they had Carlos, and I had only just one card to play and nothing to bluff with. I had paid up before and they would reason I'd pay up again. People like me always paid up.

#34

Marija's phone message on my motel phone was two parts saccharine, one part menace. It chilled me to recollect her back at the farmhouse when Tanya was breathing her last. The woman's heart for duplicity would have served her well in the social salons of Louis XIV.

I screened it the way those guys in the van would. Except for linking me to a man implicated in a recent bank robbery, and blood-related to another for the same, and both of them wanted for questioning in the kidnapping-murder of a Youngstown businessman, I was banking on Pippin not taking that tape to a grand jury and getting an indictment on me. The subtext of her message was clear –

same booth, Oak Room, same time as before, when they had run me through my drunken paces. She ended it with a sultry "Ciao!" that made me want to smash her nose into her lovely face with a ball-peen hammer.

The first job was to evade my watchers and for that I would need Stevie's help. I had paid her and then given her the remainder of my money for a week's hire.

She was happy to have it in the bundles of small denominations I laid in her lap. She held it to her nose. "Wowie, kazowie, homo pocus, motherfucker. Didja pull this out some old man's ass crack?"

"His swimming pool, actually," I said. She dropped me at the motel.

"It stinks but sure tastes good," she said and lapped her silver tongue stud against a wad of the dirty bills.

"Don't get high tonight, Stevie. I'm going to need you," I said.

"Don't you worry about me, man. You keep doing me right, I'll do you right."

After we synced watches, she drove off squealing tires. I had a brief pang of conscience for not telling her very much this time either. She was unaware of the danger of being in too close proximity to me. I was turning into my father: anybody who stooped for a blood-stained dollar deserved whatever happened. If she followed my instructions for picking me up at the spot tonight and was half as good as her brag about her driving skills, I might make the meeting without my escorts.

I paced the floor of my room. In truth, Calderone frightened me; the grotesque image of heads dumped out of a sack and lined up on a bar was the work of a man who had no boundaries and knew no fear. If they had an acoustical mic on the window pane, they'd pick up the pay-per-view sounds of soft porn and not the shuffling of my feet wearing a path in the carpet, too nerve-shot to sleep.

I splashed some water on my face and dressed in dark clothes beneath cargo pants and a white shirt. Pippin's men wouldn't need night-vision goggles to keep me in view. I practically glowed in the dark. I had a cheap pair of deck shoes with some good tread that would keep me from slip-sliding all the way down the grassy slope into a ravine at the bottom of the interstate exit.

I checked the time and left my room. I took the steps down instead of the elevator and walked out into the far back lot. I kept my hands in my pockets and slowed my pace to a walk like someone out for a stroll. A light rain was falling but it was a warm night. The cars that passed by looked bled of color in the misty glare of the orange sodium lights leading from the junction. Cars pulled ahead north and south, with a few turning off to the B & P station or one of the six fast-food places squatting in garish colors lining the exchange like grizzlies hooking steelhead.

I slowed my pace. When I reached the southern edge of the bridge abutment over the highways, I broke into a sprint. I stripped and tossed my shirt and pants as far as I could fling them under the bridge and made it to the bottom without a neck-breaking headfirst fall down the steep grassy hillside.

Forks of lightning speared the western sky. I counted twelve cars before I saw her coming, and when she pulled over to pick me up, the timing was perfect to the second. The road surface glistened with a greasy film; the light rain created a slick crud. She found a gap between a couple eighteen-wheelers and slid into it with the overworked engine of her Mazda screaming in protest.

The air brakes and horn blast of the truck in the passing lane expressed his displeasure at our sudden appearance in front of his grill. When he beamed his brights, the interior of the car lit up like a high-school stage play. I suggested she might mollify him by dropping back, but she raised a finger to the rearview mirror and provoked another crescendo from his horn.

"Stevie, I don't need any more enemies than I've got," I said.

"That motherfucker," she said.

"This is the exit," I said.

"That motherfucker," she said with an icier calm than before.

"Let it go. This is the exit, Stevie. You have to turn around right here."

Despite the banal message on my machine, Marija was giving me no leeway. If I was a minute late, I could expect her to be gone. She knew she was hot now, and nobody was under the cops' radar. She had suckered me from the very beginning, this woman. I played into her hands and licked crumbs from them. She came on Doris Day in a poodle skirt and bobbysocks, but she had a black heart beneath that Frederick's of Hollywood teddy. Any Northtown redneck would have been a greater challenge than I had proved. I couldn't blame Sarah's dumping me and wounded pride, either.

Stevie was good. She had a feather touch with her vehicle and timed the traffic lights for green all the way down 531 through Jefferson to the curve leading to the Strip. She pulled in to the Oak Room parking lot on time. She killed her headlamps and extracted the tiny overhead bulb from her shirt pocket and showed it to me.

"Now can I join the secret agent club?" She added a wink.

"Be in the parking lot in fifteen," I said.

"Lighten up, Jack, for shit's sake."

I slipped out of the dark car while it was still moving; she accelerated between a pair of parked cars. The Strip was almost deserted. Up ahead, under the lights at Little Minnesota, I saw a few rain-soaked girls cadging change. The rain kept falling and my black windbreaker was slick from brushing up against the overgrown sumac poking through fence holes by the time I opened the back doors of the Oak Room.

She was there alone with a couple drinks in front of her. She matched me in black: black Levi's, black knit sweater top, and black boots. Her breasts took up so much of the fabric that she exposed a crescent of white belly flesh when she leaned forward to scoop quarters off the bar.

I sat down and set the drink waiting for me aside. I used several cocktail napkins to wipe the rain from my face.

"I had a brother back home," she said.

"I don't give a shit about your brother."

"You're upset, aren't you?"

"Upset? Why no, Marija. Should I be?"

"Randall said you're not like him, your brother. You'd overpower me if you had the chance."

"We're here to talk about the money for my brother," I

said.

"Drink first. Take the chill off. It's a Seven-and-Seven."

"Do you know how I'd like to warm up, Marija?" I gave her a lewd grin.

"How, Jack? Tell me." She grazed the backs of my hands with her long pink fingernails. My hair was still dripping wet.

"I'd like to open you up from your neck to your navel and stick my cold hands inside your loose, warm guts."

"You're brave when he isn't around," she said. She tried to withdraw her hand from my grip.

"Is he close?" I squeezed hard.

"Oh, you like giving me pain," she leaned closer. "You want to hurt me."

"I want you to kill you, but first I want proof you have my brother." I released her hand; she didn't look at it as she pulled it back.

"A first means there's a second, Jack."

"We'll get to that later."

"Who says you're making the decisions now?"

I started to stand up but she reached a hand out to stop me.

"Sit down. Don't be an idiot," she said. "Here's what we expect you to do."

She placed a folded square of paper in front of me. I picked it up and looked at it without unfolding it. I dropped it in her drink.

"You heard what I said, Marija. Proof first."

"Proof of life? Like the movies, huh?"

"You and Calderone can say goodbye to the money. I'll blow one-third on a Lamborghini, and I'll stick the rest in the trunk before I drive it down to West Virginia and push it over a cliff."

Her stare lasered me like a cop pulling over a drunk driver.

"Look at this," she said. She had it tucked into the waistband of her jeans. I watched it ride up to expose a good portion of thong as she braced herself against the back of booth to pull it out. It was a white wash cloth folded over several times. A broken rust-colored line stained one side like snow withdrawing from a peak. I unwrapped it a fold at a time and looked at its torn edge. Carlos' earring was still attached to the lobe – a silver number fourteen.

"Don't get crazy, Jack," she said. "Randall wanted to bring you an eyeball, but I talked him out of it."

I looked at her.

"Your brother doesn't give two shits about you," she said. "He was in Buffalo before he stopped off to get high. The fool called Randall and asked him if he could come back. Can you believe? Like a bitch whimpering to be taken back by his pimp. He thought the money would smooth things over. You should have heard Randall on the phone sweet-talking him. By the way, he said he hated you and he wanted to help us kill you."

"Maybe... maybe he's got his reasons," I said.

"He's supposed to be so smart, your brother, huh? They let him have computers. That's how he came up with the idea to find a woman bank manager."

"Find the weakness," I mumbled. I was reeling from what she had said about my brother's hatred.

"Carl said your father used to make you sleep without

bed sheets in winter and kept the window open. He said it was to toughen you up."

Her words stung. "My father believed it would come in handy if we ever found ourselves floundering in a lifeboat," I said.

"It didn't work on your little brother very well, did it? He turned into a little sissy in prison. When Randall told me about him, I was the one who told him to cultivate him, even though it made him sick to his stomach – so perverted-"

I slapped her hard across the face. The sound it made stopped all conversation in the bar. The bartender began wiping down the bar closer to us. I looked at him. Marija waved him off. She fixed me with a look; her features were composed and she had a bloody smile; she dabbed her lips with a napkin.

"I knew it, Jack. You like hurting women, too," she said.

She took a swallow of her drink to wash down the blood in her mouth. Her bottom teeth were still rimed with a bloody smear. We were less than a foot apart with my brother's ear in a wash cloth between us like a gauntlet.

"Randall said you fight like a girl. He said you couldn't break an egg," she mocked.

"Tell me what you want," I said.

"When I was fourteen, four boys from Dubrovnik lured me into a house. They held me down and raped me. Because I fought them, they turned me over and sodomized me to teach me a lesson. It took me ten years to get to each one but I did it."

"And you imply I have problems with the opposite sex?"

"So what kind of freak are you, big brother? Let me

guess. I see you more as the type to break into a woman's house to sniff her panties," she said.

I had done that once in Montreal. I had done other things I didn't want to think about...

Her eyes lit up. "You like to watch. You liked watching Randall fuck me."

Her red mouth had a Halloween look.

"Deny it, Jack," she said.

"Second condition," I said and looked away from her. My voice was husky. The couple closest to us was stealing looks our way. Our conversation was unusual, even for bar talk. "We make the exchange here."

"Not here," she said. "My cabin down the street."

"I'm not going to be that stupid twice," I said.

"Yes, you are, Jack. How hard would it be for me to drop a package in the mail on my way out of town – say, a package addressed to your FBI agent – a package containing a gun used in a murder with your prints all over it?"

"They know the gunshot was postmortem," I said.

"Think about it, hero. Do you need one more piece of evidence linking you to everything?"

"*Cela ne fait rien*," I said. Something my father mumbled to himself around the apartment after my mother died. I remembered it after all these years: It doesn't matter, it doesn't matter...

"I'll have the money but not on me," I said. "When my brother walks away, you can have it. The deal includes the gun."

She smiled. "The gun's my insurance. Besides, a girl never knows when she might need protection."

She looked at me for a reaction. "You must think we're stupid like these cops letting you run around. Wait two minutes and then leave by the front door," she said. She scooped up the ear like so much loose change.

"So long, Peeping Tom," she said.

"Au revoir, you bitch," I said to her but she was too far away to hear and she knew full well I was mesmerized by the lovely movement of her backside. The old man would not have approved of showing weakness like that.

I watched her stop at the doorway and put a plastic scarf around her blonde head and walk out. I put a ten on the bar and fetched the note out of my drink with two fingers. I wasn't planning on waiting.

Stevie was slumped against the window on her side. She had a small hole in the left side of her head and a much larger one where the slug exited. I didn't see it there, but the fist-sized chunk of brain matter on the headrest and the bone fragments on the dashboard and steering wheel made further looking unnecessary. I patted down her pockets and looked under the body in case the gun with my prints was lying there.

Calderone would have used a silencer. She was probably counting it when the barrel was put to her temple. Her jaw was slack. Loose bills lay scattered in her lap. She had plenty of money now to pay the ferryman her way across the black river.

I heard a siren's wail coming from opposite ends of the strip. No matter how tough I had tried to come across inside, I was being given the same message in the parking lot: I was her monkey. She was the organ grinder.

#35

"Camera's off, Jack," Pippin said. Cops turn off cameras as often as Amish women invite lap dancers to their sewing bees. They can lie; the Supreme Court said so.

I let out a deep sigh and looked down at my hands. I twisted them around. The old man would have called it overkill, but I was so tired I wasn't acting anymore. My father lived in a time before 'deniable plausibility' became a catchphrase but the words rang in my head like a temple gong. They broke me down, I looked the part. I told them about meeting Marija in the bar and my brother's ear on the table. I even mentioned the blackmail about the gun.

"So how did your prints get on the gun, Jack?" Pippin

asked me softly. His facial expression said he was my friend, my father confessor. He practically tingled with concern. We are in this thing together, it said.

"I'm not sure," I said. "I was drunk – I remember passing out at my house. Maybe somebody came upstairs and, you know, put the gun into my hand while I was knocked out."

It was thinner than rooster soup. Pippin nodded to a second female agent taking notes. She wrote as if she had just heard the formula to convert water to gasoline.

They cut me loose at quarter to six. The lump of grease in my belly was pretty much dispersed or congealed throughout my nether regions by then to make me feel uniformly miserable. Despite the bloat, my pants were now so loose that I had to take my belt down to the last hole to keep them up.

Pippin walked me to the door.

"Was all that really necessary, Trichaud? All that sob-story jibber-jabber-"

"How long is he good for?" I interjected.

"Oh, he'll buzz me about sixteen times tonight wanting to know if we're doing the right thing by not following through on the warrant. Let's say, for your sake, if you're not waiting for me in the lobby at nine tonight, all bets are off," Pippin said.

"Thanks, Forzell."

"Thank me when it's over, gunner," he said. He pointed his finger gun at me and blew away the imaginary smoke.

The deputy who dropped me off at the motel didn't leave. He followed me up in the elevator and stood outside my door while I unlocked it. He didn't return my good night.

I went around the room collecting the articles I had secreted in various places. Desert-camo backpack, gloves, nylon rope. They found the items I had left for them in the vents and other places they were likely to check first. Nothing that would add up to anything but a red herring. I secreted everything into my clothing about me.

The red light on my phone blinked on and off. It was Sarah.

"I don't want to leave a message," she said. "I want to know why you gave me that thing." She meant the Guardian Angel, which had a sticky red label across the back that said 'nonlethal device.' I was glad I hadn't been there to answer the phone because I had nothing more than my intuition to explain it.

I threw the curtains aside and opened the windows. The drop was twenty feet to a grassy verge that would break my fall, worst case, but that would simply put me in front of the headlights of the surveillance car. I needed to get to the roof to have any chance.

The jump across my balcony to the next one was just five feet. I looked out over the lot and took in the surveillance teams below. The leap would land me on the railing, and I had a feeling that I was going to end up with a broken neck like some drunken college kid on spring break. I had to snag one of the overhanging faux beams that stuck out from the roof at intervals for whatever the esthetic effect these lent to architecture that was mindlessly utilitarian – a rectangle with a couple smaller squares fore and aft.

I had a stomach-churning fear the beam would turn out

to be hollow plaster tubing and explode in my hands and I'd go into the dirt below like a dart or land on the cement balcony of the floor below me. The thin aluminum railing wasn't much for stability, either, and I would need to extend my hands high above my head when I jumped.

I jumped and my grip on the beam was nothing short of cadaveric. I waited for my body to stop swinging like a pendulum for the final move. Below me, I heard car doors slam, men's shouts, and feet running across the parking lot. They were sitting in their cars too long, watching my little Cirque de Soleil stunt, and this was going to get them reamed by Pippin.

When I was still enough, I swung my foot up high and hard to clear the lip of the roof. My shoe caught in the middle of my instep but slipped from the tarred roof. I hadn't expected that. Now I was hanging straight down and weaker for the effort.

I sucked in my breath and swung my legs again – this time I overshot and my heel bounced a couple of times along the edge and then slid off with the same result except that my upper body and my arms were now quivering from strain.

The third swing did it. I made it perfect and kept the momentum to roll my weight up and over the beam. I lay gasping on the roof while my lungs recovered. I was in such weakened condition from fatigue that my legs and arms continued to twitch. I lay there wheezing like a ninety-year-old man with asthma. My mind drifted to a time I had taken Carlos with me on one of my jaunts in Montreal – a stupid thing but I was vain of my prowess and roofs were my strong suit. I had Carlos in an overlapping handhold and was hoisting him up from a third-story landing at the very moment a security guard passed directly below us. I held Carlos above his head; my hands locked around his in a vise grip. I remembered staring at the glowing orange tip of his cigarette and focusing on that, watching it shrink until he finally stubbed it out against the side of the building. When I pulled Carlos up to me, his face was white. We never spoke about that escapade of amateur terror, but my muscles had stored it in memory.

I forced myself to get up. I couldn't run well because my leg muscles were shaking. I made it to the opposite side of the roof from where Pippin's agents spotted me.

I removed the rope and gloves. I made a slipknot and threw the end of the rope over a beam projecting out from the end of the building. The leather gloves were thick but not exactly the kind Delta soldiers used to repel out of Black Hawks. I had no idea if this was going to work right, but I made my second leap of faith off the building and within seconds I was plummeting in a controlled fall toward the grass below. My hands began to heat up from the sizzling friction burn but it didn't get unbearable until I was just a few feet from the ground.

All of this from balcony through the swing upward to the roof to the rope trick didn't consume more than a few minutes, but if I was spotted by Pippin's men now it would all have been for nothing. They had to be tearing around the upper floor looking for a way to the roof. I scrambled up the grassy verge and crawled over the guardrail. In seconds I was in a fast trot across the street where I ran along the culvert and made a beeline for the gas station.

I called the same cab service from the pay phone outside the gas station and told the dispatcher where his cabbie could pick me up. I had a quarter-mile run from there to the Clay Street Inn where the cab would meet me. But I had no more than an hour to talk the driver into riding me free down to the beach. I still had to hope this person would be willing to forego common sense and wait while I scampered along the flat rocks another quarter mile to retrieve the money. For all I knew, some lucky fisherman had snagged the bag on his line fishing for sheepshead and carp. Then I had to get this cabbie to fly at breakneck speed to Marija's cabin at Jefferson-on-the-Lake and hope that no cops or state troopers were passing the other way on shift change.

For every minute late, the sodden note said, another part of Carlos would be deducted. It was full of misspellings and signed 'Gess Hoo.'

#36

Luck takes different forms in life. Sometimes it's the right people you meet at the right time, and then everything changes for the good. Sometimes it's just you imposing your will in some kind of way that accords with quantum physics and the universe respects your decision. The driver they sent me was not only willing to forego common sense but he had left it behind in some previous incarnation. He was about twenty-five, had a light sheen on his forehead and tiny red spots from picking – a meth head chasing invisible crank bugs beneath the skin. Anyone halfway normal would have sped off and left me standing there. He had the outline of a skull tattooed on the back of his head;

his hands bore the fine blue etching of each knuckle bone laid atop the skin of all his fingers. He drove wildly fast and passed cars down recklessly. He talked nonstop about his out-of-body meditation experiences and asked me, innocently, if I thought he was crazy.

He pulled up so close to the breakwall that I thought his bumper was going to hit the green handrail to the aluminum steps the city had leaned against it. Waves were pounding the other side of the wall and a plume of water hit the hood of his cab.

"Fucking sand," he glowed. "I love this shit."

"Here's half the money, as promised," I said. "The other half when I get back."

He stared straight ahead at the massive rocks, apparently caught up in some memory of sand doing something to him somewhere. I took the heavy aluminum steps two at a time and raced down the rocks toward the stubby lighthouse at the mouth of the harbor.

There wasn't a fisherman to be seen because of the chop. That was all the luck I was going to have. What appeared from my backyard to be a dun-colored arrow of round boulders was a broken, uneven surface slickened to ice by the crashing waves and strewn with puddles of algae-covered slime.

I ran like a badly intoxicated drunk taking a field sobriety test blindfolded. The gaps between the rocks were impossible to negotiate at one speed – run too fast and I'd stumble headfirst over the side, hit a patch of seaweed and the result would be a pratfall that would crack my skull open like a rotten melon. I aimed for the lighthouse and tried to keep my footsteps on course, but I was soon flailing my arms and my head was bouncing on the stem of my neck like a Barbie doll as the rocks slipped out from under me.

The exact configuration where I stashed the bag was a memory imprint from the time I put it inside the fissure. I love angles, and every combination of the granite shapes was unique. I ran on harder, getting better footing and fought off the chill creeping up my spine that said I wouldn't recognize it in this half-crazed condition. I'd be that guy in the book of fairy tales who couldn't remember which tree he buried the gold under.

The one thing I hadn't factored in was the seven-foot waves rolling in from the northwest fetch. The bag was waterproof but I wasn't. I had to climb halfway down to get to the crack; the waves came fast in intervals like the flank of a charging battalion. I was already soaked from the spray hitting me as I ran. Now I had to time it so that I could reach my entire arm inside the pocket. The lower portion of the rocks on the lakeside was normally exposed to the lake's invisible progress toward Niagara Falls. The ebb of the withdrawing waves left the lower rocks exposed down to their mantle of green seaweed.

The trick was to get my body down there and flatten myself before the first wave hit. Then I had to stick my arm through the crevice and find the bag with my fingers. If I didn't pull it out in time, the incoming water might knock me from my perch, and then I'd be scrabbling about fully clothed in the surf. I would have to take at least one breaking wave over my body and get out of there before the next one caught me. I would be underwater for part of this.

My mind locked on to it exactly as it had during my trek down the wall yesterday afternoon. It was fifty yards off from the spot. Just as I reached the rock where I had to make my first move, a big comber rolled in and showered me with a pelting spray. It was like someone standing in front of me and hurling a bucket of water into my face.

By the time I cleared my eyes the next wave, not as high, was already cresting on its heels. Churned up water spread all the way to the black horizon and boiled up from an inky base of clouds that dipped down to touch the water. My courage evaporated like smoke while I stood there letting the seconds pass; my legs remained bolted to the granite surface. I cursed my father's bones. Not a scintilla of light or hope was possible in this surreal disaster. When I was young, even in the worst of it, I still clung to the hope that I was going to have a real life despite my father's dementia – it poked up like a blade of grass through cement no matter how depressing things were getting at home.

"God damn you motherfuckers," I said to the waves, but I meant everybody: my sick father, my twisted brother, my faithless wife, and that pair of amoral sexual degenerates who picked me out of a city directory like God pointing his finger at one luckless pismire whose day of wrath was at hand. I wanted the water to knock me off the wall and drown me. I had hit bottom and stood with a dumb bovine look on my face, if anybody cared to see it, just standing there inert gaping at a black sky. The water surged back and forth, in and out, back and forth, elements copulating, making geysers all around my half-frozen legs.

"Fuck it," I said. I scrambled down like a water spider

before the next wave swept in. I found toeholds and handholds among the crevices. I flattened myself as well as possible and let the onrushing mass of water pound me in a frothy surf. I was completely soaked and shocked by the cold. The bathwater temperatures of summer were gone, and I felt the chill into the marrow of my bones. I reached into the hole and thrashed my arm through the foamy backwash. Nothing. I was taking too long – another wave was due. I pulled back just in time and reclaimed my position before the next wave smacked me somewhere around the kidneys and almost pried me loose.

While I was still underwater, I thrust my arm into the hole again and this time I touched fabric. My fingers slipped around on it and I had enough of it to dislodge when a wave unexpectedly took me with twice the force of the last one. I was lifted like a mother cat picking up a kitten by the nape. This time there was no holding on to the rocks and the bag was too heavy to manage in the crashing surf. My body loosened, slipped, and then I was rolling in the water. It had the force of a rip tide and pulled me back into the lake away from the rocks.

I was treading water anchored to a bag of money about ten yards from where I had gone in. I turned my head in time to see the curl right over me and dove down to avoid it. The bag was so cumbersome I didn't get far under before the wave broke over my back. The surf this close was so wild and full of rogue waves and backflow from the rocks that the air I tried to breathe was saturated with flying water.

I turned over and floated on my back, dragging my boat anchor, and kicked as hard as I could in my sodden clothes. I made little progress and could see nothing but foamy water and feel the undulations carrying me every way but toward the rocks.

My strength was expended just to maintain my head above the water and my scissoring legs starting to go lower and lower into the heavy tide. My lungs burned. I knew I had to let go of the money to save my life...

A big wave took me down beneath the surface, and I felt the blackness slip around my vision and replace the dirty green murk. I was becoming light-headed. I had a thought of letting go but something appeared at the periphery of my vision – or maybe I was seeing something caused by the changing blood pressure in my head. I saw foamy white ribbons, small vortexes like tiny tornadoes against the black. I swam for them.

My body went into the rocks and I felt the shock in my hip through the churning water. I gulped a mouthful of the brackish water when my head cleared the surface. The next wave vaulted me higher and I was able to get a purchase with my one hand on the slimy rocks. I hung there resting until I had enough strength and air to climb higher. My soaked clothes and shoes weighed me down.

The gods who love a joke didn't want it to end here, however. As soon as I was able to roll over and vomit out some of the brackish water, I spotted the backpack jammed into the rocks just feet from where I had climbed up; it lay tucked into the surf like an abandoned baby seal with water breaking all around it and bubbling up from the cracks. I cupped my fingers like a rock climber and lowered myself down to it. One wrong move over the seaweed-covered rocks and the mocking gods would send me down a greased chute back into the water.

I eased it from the crevice where it had lodged tight into a gap between the rocks. The backpack felt heavier than bricks. My shoulders and legs and side all ached. I staggered, walked, tripped and ran back the way I had come. My watch said I had chewed up eight of the forty-three minutes left before pieces of Carlos started coming off. I felt as if I had been in the water for an hour.

My mind bumped along down the breakwall with my uncooperative body. Nothing made sense, not the elixir of sex and sadism that fed Calderone and Marija. I couldn't picture any human being chopping up another like hacking through a row of cabbages. I sloshed water with every step and sucked air. My father's mocking voice came rushing back like the tinnitus in my ears and the blood finding its equilibrium in my veins: *Man is a wolf to man.*

#37

Bones, my new cabbie's street name, made it by eleven seconds. I stepped out of the cab in front of Marija's cabin, my old peeping-tom haunt, and walked down the middle of the gravel drive. No one was in sight. No tourists and all the businesses seemed rolled up for the season. I saw the shop where Marija had first flirted with me a month and a lifetime ago.

The last cabin on the right was the manager's. I skirted close enough to the window to see a bearded man dozing in a chair behind a desk. He was the one who had looked at me dropping the rope with the bags over the edge.

I pushed the door in, half-expecting to die in a hail of

bullets or to see Calderone slavering, a machete in his fist. Marija sat on a corner of the bed with her hands folded demurely in her lap. She wore something with sequins and frilly at the neck that reminded me of those ornate Elizabethan neck ruffs. She looked dressed for church.

"Well done, Jack," she said and checked a thin gold watch on her wrist. "Right on the dot. Your brother's children will thank you someday for allowing him to keep his balls."

"Why doesn't it surprise me that you'd start with those?"

She smoothed her skirt. "You might have picked a better time to go swimming."

"Where's my brother?"

"He's in the back with Randall," she said. She hiked a leg over a knee and gave me one of those smiles that had lured me in like so many other gullible fish. But it wasn't the smile I knew; this one was different, and that difference told me everything.

"Tell him to come out, I want to see him," I said.

"The money first," she said. The smile flickered a little brighter but died faster.

I dropped the backpack down at her feet. "It's mostly all there," I said. "I used some for cab fare the last couple of days."

"How much?"

"About five thousand."

"Generous, aren't you?" She didn't make a move from the bed to check it.

"I believe in tipping the working people."

"Randall would say that's mighty white of you," she

simpered. Despite the effort, she gave off fear in waves. She was in terror – not of me but of betraying him.

"What are we waiting for? Let's do this," I said.

"I forgot to mention one little detail back at the bar," she said and shifted her butt on the bed.

"Tell me," I said. The adrenalin was practically levitating me off the floor. Then I heard a muffled voice in the back room telling Carl to shut up, he'd be free in a minute.

"You're part of this, Jack. The money and you for your brother," she said. She had the gun out from beneath her lap and was pointing it at my stomach.

"I want to see my brother, Marija. Call it a request," I said.

"Turn around and lift up your shirt all the way. Do it. Or I will shoot you in the guts."

I turned around with my hands raised to my shoulders.

"Unzip the bag. If there's anything in there but money, you'll be begging me to kill you."

I kneeled down, a supplicant approaching Shiva with an offering. I unzipped it and held it open by the edges for her to see inside. "All there but my generous tip," I said.

I was staring at her, and though the gun was pointing at my chin, she cast her eyes down once, briefly, drawn by the money or to avoid acknowledging the look in my eyes that said I knew she was scamming me and that my brother was most likely dead.

"Get away from the bag," she said.

"I just want you to see it's all there. Look for yourself," I said.

She wasn't close enough yet.

"You know he's going to rip your fucking heart out," I said quietly.

She reacted to that by thrusting her free hand within range of the bag and when she did that I made my move with the concealed machete knife. The confident look on her face was still there as I rocked back on my heels as if I were frightened by the gun so close to my face. The short arc of my swing got a little torque with my hips, like a hard right hand punch to the liver – a finishing punch. The heavy blade snicked through the wrist bone but didn't sever. I cut through enough tendons to make that hand useless, but the gun in her good hand was the problem. The shock of what I did was more than enough to trip the three pounds of pressure she needed to squeeze off a round. The bullet missed me by a country mile.

I had her gun hand clenched hard in my fist. A spouting artery showered us with blood. I had my whole body on top of her and with my knife, held up only by her slapping, weakened efforts, I could easily have slit her throat. Her eyes rolled around as she tried to make sense of what was happening. I gripped the wet stump of her wrist so hard I must have stanched some of the blood flow, but her whole arm was slick with it. By the time she stopped writhing beneath me, we were both covered. It spattered everything – the bedspread, me, and dotted her face with silly red freckles.

"What you- What you always wanted, Jack," she said and gave me a sick smile. Her eyes rolled back completely and I felt her body go limp in a dead faint.

I got up slowly, not willing to take my eyes off her. Her arm hung off the side of the small bed and the ragged claw of her hand kept bleeding out into a puddle. Her breasts lay flattened against her chest and puffed out the fabric at the sides. I cut a section of blouse and tore it to make a tourniquet. Her skin was rapidly fading from bronzed to translucent. I didn't need to tie her up.

The gun rested against the wall. I recognized it as one of the 9 mms from the pile on the table in the farmhouse. I was afraid she'd bleed to death while I looked in the other room.

It was silent. I suppose that was what first told me Calderone was nowhere around this cabin. Old habit took over, I assumed the Weaver stance the old man always insisted on. Adrenalin was choking me and a vein pounded in my neck.

I lowered the gun and stuck it in my pocket. I went in low and made out a dark shape on the floor. Next to it was a cheap boxy-looking tape recorder from decades before computer chips were invented; it was still in the play position.

The shape, of course, was my brother.

It wasn't possible to tell right away because of the dim lighting and the blankets thrown over the window opposite the bed. He lay on a rubber mat, but he had been dissected elsewhere. There wasn't much blood and the coppery smell was too faint. They had done a lot of damage to his head first. The bruises were fresh, livid, but the blood had dried and oxidized to a rusty brown. The smeary blue iris of eyeballs. His torso was swathed in a bloody rag, which I realized was a dress with some kind of print. The other parts of him were stacked together: legs, arms, hands, genitalia, feet – parts for assembling a doll-man. I touched his blanched, empty face and tried to stroke his hair, but my hand was shaking too hard.

What had made him want to crawl back to Calderone? Had my father so destroyed him that he knew nothing else but to hide beneath the wing of a monster? I was no shrink, but I was guilty for this horror. When he needed me, I abandoned him. I never saw how broken he was in his mind.

When I came back into the room for her, she was gone. The bed was rumpled, bloody, and a yard-wide viscid trail of crimson showed me the way she fled as obviously as neon signs. Bloody and maimed, she had still hauled off with the backpack. I almost admired her.

I picked up my machete knife and went looking. The blood led across the porch and over the gravel road to the manager's cabin. The splatters of blood were huge red comet tails. I stuck the gun in my pants.

The manager never moved in his chair when I kicked his door. Walking past his unmoving form, I understood why: he had received the same treatment as Stevie. A splotch of dark gore and drying blood created a grim rosette on the wall. I didn't see it when I walked past him outside.

I followed the blood down his hallway and out the back door. She dropped the bag at that point because the ground was disturbed off the back steps where she must have stumbled. The drops were fewer but so plentiful that a blind man could track her. I was unaware of anything around me. Her steps showed her backtracking, wasting time and what strength she had left.

I saw the backpack ahead lying in some tall grass in a

vacant lot. A two-story building with flaking paint rose up just beyond that, a beverage shop. She was crawling on her knees through the scrub. Her bad hand was jammed tight into her side to staunch the blood flow. I could see white bone sticking out. She was about ten feet from the driveway of the building. I circled ahead and let her crawl toward me. When she noticed my legs in front of her, she stopped like a dumb animal. Her bloody hand was dangling at her side, worsened by the exertions of her escape.

She gurgled something in her throat.

"I can't hear you, Marija," I said. "You'll have to speak up."

Her frilled blouse was in tatters and exposed her breast flesh. Her hair was disheveled and had bits of moss and twigs; her face was ghostly white. The place where she had tried to hold her wound to her side was a red sopping mess. Only her eyes retained that marvelous collage of color.

I grabbed her hair and lifted her head.

"Look at me," I said.

"H-help me," she whispered.

I used the edge of my blade to cut the remnants of her dress and blouse free. I jerked the lacy ruff of her blouse so that the last buttons popped and flew.

"You want me to help you," I said.

"Help- help me," she said. The skin of her face had a doughy pallor.

"Know-you-help m-me," she said.

I stood up and looked around. There were people walking not more than forty yards from where I stood in the weeds. I couldn't hear them, but I was visible to them if they wanted to see me. Maybe I looked like a man walking his dog in a field. She was like a big dog with weak hips. I could have picked her up and turned her around and told her to go the other way. Surreal.

"Where is he, Marija?"

"House," she managed.

"Say it again," I said.

She murmured softly, "H-Help me, please." She tried to look up at me, but it was difficult for her. She shook her head from side to side like a jungle creature sipping at the water's edge leery of some big reptile exploding out of the water.

I put the blade on her lower lip and opened her mouth with it. It cut her lips when she tried to shake it out. Her eyes were losing their luster.

"Marija," I said. "Can you hear me?"

"Mmmmmmuh," she mumbled.

"Marija, listen to me. Don't faint."

She collapsed to the ground. The front of her was wet with fresh blood and her swaying breasts were painted with it.

"Don't pass out," I said. "I'll help you."

She tried to push me away with her useless hand. I saw the white bone beneath the flap of skin.

"Marija," I said. "Look at me!" I grabbed her cheeks in one hand and squeezed until her eyes bulged. "Where is Calderone?"

She made swallowing sounds. I shook her head hard. "Tell me!"

"Say again, Marija."

She spat blood with the fricatives: "Your wife... houf... her house."

Sarah's house-

"That's a good girl," I said. "Help is coming."

I sliced one corner of her mouth and then the other, which gave her a wide clown mouth. I wiped the handle of the blade around a piece of her torn skirt. I pressed the knife into her good hand. I made her look at me. I think she heard me.

"You're ugly now, Marija. Use this."

I was aware of a voice in the distance. Someone was walking toward me across the field. He stopped short and his eyes bulged when he saw her lying on her side clutching a knife and moaning. I turned away just as she evacuated her bowels noisily. More people were gathering on the sidewalk.

I picked up the backpack. I walked through the manager's cabin, past his dead body, and out the door. I was on the sidewalk. I heard shouting and I could see people speaking into cell phones.

I checked my watch. It was twenty-eight minutes since Bones had dropped me off and was waiting for me at the Oak Room. If I didn't show in a half-hour, I said, have a brew on me and go home. The street was picking up the excitement; people were running from across the street to join the commotion. I heard a young girl's falsetto scream. I kept walking.

Bones was on the hood of his cab reading a paperback edition of Steppenwolf. I threw the backpack in the back seat and climbed inside. I sat on my hands to keep the shaking down, although I knew my driver well enough to know that I was well within the range of normal to attract concern. His eyes took me in with a single glance and his face wore his reading expression.

"How was your friend?" he asked me.

"She was fine," I said. I stifled a sob with a coughing sound.

The amenities over, he said, "Hesse, man. He's all fucked up."

I couldn't tell if he meant that as a compliment. "Bones, I've got one more place to go and I need you to get me there fast."

"Where we goin' and how much you payin'?"

I gave him directions.

"We just came from there, man," Bones said.

"I'm aware of that."

"Same rules? Off the clock and you pay the tickets?"

When we passed the scene, a huge crowd had materialized from nowhere. A dozen people had their cell phones out. More were arriving from across the street, all drawn by the spell of a morbid rumor, which would turn out to be true. I saw some holding up their videophones and tablets to film it – she, the blood-soaked woman on the ground.

Ambulances and police cars were lining up. I lowered myself in the seat because Pippin's Navigator flew around the curve; we passed so close I could see he'd shaved haphazardly that day. I don't know why I suddenly had a powerful urge to talk. I gabbled nonsense about drinking beers out there with my wife when we were first married.

"Beer is for pigs," Bones said. He hit the gas once we left the resort town behind.

I was lost in synaptic misfirings of the brain, unable to think, unable to come to grips with the brute inside who had done what I had just done to a beautiful woman I once desired. I heard Bones ask what the excitement was back at Jefferson-on-the-Lake.

"God knows," I said. "God knows."

FRIDAY, SEPTEMBER 10

9:05 P.M.

#38

There's nothing really safe in the world. Evil stops here and there for a while, but it's always on the move and able to come to you wherever you are. It's when you stand still too long that you make the best target.

I saw my wife's head through the kitchen window. She was doing the supper dishes. Behind me a mile out from the breakwall, deck lights from a thousand-footer, a massive ore carrier, glowed in the blackness like a string of Japanese lanterns. Waves flashed white where they broke over the bow and rolled along against the side of the hull amidships before they disappeared. Sine, cosine, tangent – all the angles of life were at play out there in the water buffeting the steel.

Sarah would go into the living room soon and watch television after the dishes. It's what she always did. My teeth chattered, but it wasn't from chilled air sucked across the open lake water. I had spent the last several hours lurking in my garage behind plastic drop cloths.

The lights in the houses went out and porch lights came on. The blue phosphorescent glow of television sets in living rooms up and down the neighborhood shone through half-drawn curtains and windows. Sarah watched the news before going to bed. Her boyfriend's truck was parked behind her car in the driveway. I had not seen him appear in any windows yet. Something else I would have missed if I had turned my head a mere second later. A dark shape left the back seat just as the driver pulled up to the curb three houses down. This shape was a man who ran to an oak tree and then disappeared at a fast trot down the driveway of an older couple who manicured their lawns. The shape wasn't just a man; it was a large man who ran like a panther, and only one name to attach to the vision: Gess Hoo himself coming to visit.

I couldn't see him clearly because of the darkness, but I had my eyes fixed on a spot near the far end where he'd have to come out. He'd want to circle this way. I was sure that the slightest shift in the black would tell me when he made a move.

That's when I heard the garage door swing on its rail. I had my hand inside my pants for the automatic, but his beam blinded me. Sarah's boyfriend didn't shout; he wasn't going to scare me that way. What did was his other hand on the trigger of a twenty-gauge that was poking through the garage doors at my chest.

"Don't fucking move a muscle," he said through his teeth.

"It's Trichaud," I said. "Listen, I'm not here to-"

"Shut up."

"You need to hear me, please," I begged.

"Shut your mouth, asshole. I've got you now," he gloated.

"Listen, Sarah's in danger. You're in danger. There's a man-"

His voice was raspy, and I didn't want to provoke him in case he was one of those stand-your-ground types. At this range, I'd have the wadding embedded in my spine along with any pellets that didn't punch through me on their way out my back.

He muscled himself through the doors to get all the way in. I couldn't watch. I closed my eyes at the expected blast from his finger accidentally squeezing the trigger.

"I won't move. Please don't put the light on," I said. "There's someone out there who-"

"You brought someone?"

He tossed the flashlight aside and held the twenty-gauge tighter against his shoulder.

"Don't turn on the light."

"And you're carrying a gun, you crazy fuck? You brought a fucking gun here?"

He shoved the tip of the barrel at me so hard I fell back against a tool cabinet.

"You move, you die," he said.

I hoped I could talk him round to the greater danger out in the dark who had to be listening to this exchange.

When he lowered the barrel to take the gun out of my belt I had a chance, but I let it go. He shoved it into his back pocket and stepped back.

Worse always comes to worse: he hit the light switch.

I tried once more. "Look, Sarah will tell you-"

"You're stalking her, Trichaud," he said.

"No, listen to me. There's a very, very bad individual out there who's watching us right now and he has a gun-"

"Move!"

I got up and held my hands in the air. He put the barrel into my right shoulder blade and marched me outside.

"This is good, Trichaud," he said; "you're going to prison for a long time. I could shoot you right here and the law would pin a medal on me."

I knew at least one FBI agent who would have vied with him for that honor. My thoughts were bent in one direction: to get indoors where wood and brick might save me from the wolf.

"Call the cops," I said.

"Shut the fuck up, Trichaud. What did she ever see in an asshole like you?"

"Let's go inside and I'll tell you everything."

My heart was thumping like a bellows. Calderone wasn't going to wait for the cops to come.

"You're in a big hurry to get to prison, huh?" He nudged me off the back steps with his shotgun.

It was too long a walk down the dark driveway. I looked at the vehicles and saw big trouble. I took a huge chance and stopped. "Just listen to me for one second," I pleaded.

He clipped me across the jaw with the barrel.

When I reached the gap between the vehicles, I was

going to make a move no matter what. I was too late. I didn't hear the whistle of the bat descending in an arc on his skull, but the crack registered obviously enough.

I didn't wait for the next swing. I was off and running in an all-out sprint. I flew past the rose trellis at the corner of the house like a downhill skier. Even in the dusk, I knew to the inch how wide to take the corner-

But I stopped all my forward momentum when I saw the second shotgun.

"Waitin' for you, Jack," the man holding it said. "Let's go in. Someone wants to meet you."

Lights were beginning to come on in some of the houses. Life was behaving normally as day was replaced by night in my once-calm neighborhood.

He walked me back the way I had just come, my rabbit's heart pounding in my throat, and saw Sarah's boyfriend lying at the edge of the driveway where he had dropped like a manhole cover. He was on his back but his knees were buckled as if he had fallen backward. His rolled-up white eyeballs were all I needed to know.

The light was murky as last night's dishwater; yard spiders' webs glowed like patches of dirty cotton candy in the green grass. We walked through the porch into the kitchen. The drawers were full of knives within hand's reach and a galaxy away. I could see my father shaking his head mournfully: Bringing a knife to a gunfight, Jackie? That's not smart.

"Nothing I've done yet has been," I said as we moved through to the sitting room.

"Don't talk, motherfucker," he said. "Randy says if you run, I can blow your knee caps off."

I lost what little composure I had left. I weaved into an octagon table sticking out from the couch and sent glass candle holders flying onto the carpet. He pushed me with his shotgun toward the stairway banister. I stumbled up, a straggler on the Bataan Death March. He stayed a foot behind me with a hard prod to the kidneys if I didn't go fast enough.

Big, mean Randall Calderone stood at the top of the stairs. "I been waitin' on you," he said. No glee, no malice, just a psychopath's greeting. He wore the black leather vest he had on the first time I saw him. The bulked-up arms and prison tatts, the pointy goatee and the bald head. All the same as if no time at all had passed.

Calderone took a quick stride toward me. He bit off the edge of some duct tape he had been wrapping his hand in and punched me on the jaw. It wasn't meant to be a knockout, just a way of showing me his power. I knew he had more interesting plans for me than a mere beating to death with his fists.

Like so many other experiences from my two-week sojourn through hell, it was one more circle of the inferno to discover. He dragged me into the bedroom. I heard sniffling and whimpering coming from the opposite corner; she was gagged, nude, lying on the bed and imploring me with her eyes. I had no explanation to give her for the question I read so easily: Why? Why was this happening?

Calderone and his partner were talking loudly through the doorway. Calderone wanted to begin dicing me up like my brother. The other man wanted to get the money, as Calderone had apparently promised him. They kept calling each other "bro." Biker brothers, Aryan brotherhood, whatever it was, I wasn't going to be asked for my opinion.

"He ain't got it here, bro," Calderone said. "You'd a seen it in the garage."

The other man said, "Fuckin' newspaper said bills was found out there with her, man. Couple hundred bucks lying around in the field where they found her."

"Maybe some motherfucker picked it up before the cops came," Calderone said.

"You don't know that for sure, Randall. Bitch wakes up, it'll be in a prison hospital and she ain't gonna remember shit."

Marija alive.

"Man, you start cutting him up..." He stopped pacing between the two rooms, looking down at me nervously. When he noticed me awake, listening, they moved off into the other room. It felt as if a ball of ice had been thrust into my rib cage, replacing my heart. Nothing quite like hearing your own murder being discussed in front of you.

Sarah looked at me. Her eyes told me she took in every word of their talk as well.

We heard footsteps coming down the hallway. Calderone appeared in front of me staring down; his hands on his hips and he had that grin I remembered from the first day. He jerked me upright to a sitting position. Then he reared back and kicked me in the face so hard I flew backwards into the bed.

"You fucking fuck," he said. "This was so fucking simple. We had the fucking money, and all you had to do was follow the plan." His grin was an icy leer. "I'm gonna do ten times worse to that bitch what you did to Marija."

He dropped a newspaper in front of me and left. I had to twist my head to read it.

> An unidentified woman in her mid-twenties was found partially nude in a field with severe wounds, including an amputated hand, in a deserted lot at Jefferson-on-the-Lake. The small resort town is located midway between Cleveland and Erie, PA...

I couldn't read the bottom half of it because part of my face was swelling up. The middle portion was clear enough to make out:

> Police also found the manager of Pineywood Log Cabins, Buck Frontenatta, aged forty-three, shot to death in his office. Frontenatta was once a leader of the Cleveland chapter of the Hell's Angels back in the early nineteen-nineties. His body was sent to Cuyahoga County Medical Examiner's office where pathologist Elizabeth Bhargrava is performing the autopsy. The woman, whose left hand was almost completely severed, was flown by emergency helicopter evacuation to St. Elizabeth's hospital in Youngstown. A police spokesman said they are currently investigating leads but have no comment at this time. FBI Agent Forzell Pippin-

Footsteps were approaching. Calderone and his partner

came back. He picked up the paper and frowned. He pointed a thick finger at the article's column. He read like a child whose fate was always to be in the last group stigmatized for its stupidity:

"'Forzell Pippin had no comment at this time but said the' – said the – 'multi-agency task force is investigating all leads.'"

"That means the cops are heading here soon," I said. "You and your friend should leave now."

I thought he was about to kick me in the face again. "I've got the money," I said; "it's very close by – maybe a mile. Almost the full nine hundred thous-"

This time he did kick me. I deflected most of its force by twisting my head. I fought for air for what seemed an eternity of minutes that stretched into hours and days that produced no oxygen in my burning lungs.

"It ain't right, bro," the other one muttered. "I'm takin' the same chances as you."

"Shut the fuck up and let me think," Calderone snapped.

This man wasn't Calderone's size and his two-hundred-eighty or ninety pounds were mostly flab. His arms and belly stretched the fabric of his black tee-shirt and his wrists were as thick as barge poles.

"Come on, man. Let's drill this bitch and go get us the money," he said.

I couldn't talk yet, the sounds were hoarse coming as they did from a damaged larynx, but I managed the word No all right.

"No, what, you fuckface cunt?"

Calderone peered down at me between the single line of

his black eyebrow and put a boot on my forehead. He looked about to launch a fist at me so I squeezed my head into my neck and hoped he shattered every metacarpal bone in his hand.

"Wait, Randy!" The fat one grabbed Calderone by his wrist. "Let's hear this shitsucker out, bro," he said.

"No-money-hurt-her," I managed to wheeze out.

Calderone was torn between beating me to death and getting his hands on the money – a boon he must have thought would never come his way after the discovery of Marija's body in the field and the money missing. Revenge was on hold for greed, for the moment.

He leaned over me. "Your faggot brother died screaming. That will seem like dyin' in a four-poster bed compared to what I will do to you. Do you understand?"

"I understand." I half-coughed it.

"Where is the money?"

"Fuck's sweet sake, let the motherfucker answer," Fat Boy said.

I spoke one word and waited.

"'Break' – what the fucking hell is a breakwall?" Fat Boy shouted to Calderone.

"See that, out the window there, you dumb Kentucky hillbilly?"

Calderone pointed just beyond Sarah's still body. She could have been posing for a nude portrait with her blonde pubis shaved into a wedge, no doubt for the benefit of the latest carcass occupying my garage; she hadn't moved anything but her eyes the whole time.

Fat Boy asked Calderone to cut my hands free. They gave me a paper and pencil and I wrote down the location with simple directions. I added a crude sketch that included the house, the breakwall, and an X-marks-the spot just like a kid's pirate treasure map.

I looked at Sarah and saw the tears coursing down her cheeks. How could I ask forgiveness for the bomb crater of my life?

Calderone and Fat Boy bickered like an old married couple; neither one wanted to be left here while the other one went for the money. In the end, Calderone yielded to Fat Boy, who was going to lead me down there to fetch the bag. Calderone would remain with Sarah.

The fact that Calderone yielded to his partner and was going to let him touch all that cash told me as surely as anything else Calderone had said or done that he was setting him up. Fat Boy didn't know it, but he was going to join Sarah's man in the garage.

#39

I wasn't taking a chance with Sarah's life. I located the bag easily enough. Fat Boy made me carry it back to the car. When I tried to tell him what Calderone intended for him, he backhanded me across the face.

Two hours later, at the height of his glee, while he was counting out the bills on my living room floor, Calderone put a bullet in his head without so much as a harsh word or a whisper.

I saw Fat Boy's boots wobble in front of me – a couple inches forward and then a stutter-step backward a couple more inches like someone anticipating a dance move. He fell hard and slammed all his weight into the floor; it shook the room and rattled the tiny crystals hanging from Sarah's lamps.

Fat Boy's eyes stayed wide open. His face was mere inches from mine as I lay trussed near the sofa. The tiny red hole in the center of his forehead wasn't big enough for my pinkie to fit into.

Calderone, standing above me, said quietly, "You can run punks in the joint, but you don't keep them. Brotherhood rules, man. I told him that a dozen times."

I heard the sound of the silencer being unscrewed from the barrel. He dropped it on the floor where smoke curled out of drilled holes. He patted Fat Boy down and removed the Taurus from the back of Fat Boy's pants. He circled his left boot with his hands and went up it to his calf. He found a little Phoenix Arms .25 in his right boot. He worked the slide and ejected a shell. He held it out in front of my face.

"Now what you suppose my bro intended to do with this?" He rolled me over so I could see him.

"Ho-hum," Calderone said with a big yawn and a stretch. "I think I'll go upstairs and fuck the wife."

He put his boot on my neck and rocked all his body weight in to it. After the third time, I thought my eyeballs were going to pop out of my head.

"No point in squirming, Jack-off. You keep my man company down here because I ain't lugging your ass up those stairs. Your wife's name, remind me."

"Sarah," I said. "Her name is Sarah. Please don't hurt her."

"Sarah. A Jew, huh? Don't matter. She reminds me of this strung-out little girl in Albuquerque. Used to squirt her pussy juice all over me when she came. She liked it in the ass. Bet you there's a lot she's gonna learn from me you never showed her, flower boy."

He tossed the rest of the spilled packets of money into the backpack. He went over each of Fat Boy's knots on my hands and feet. When he was satisfied with the tension on the cords, he picked up the backpack by a strap.

"All them books with big words upstairs ain't gonna help you or her. I didn't need books down in Mexico. You learn by doing down there."

"Calderone, listen to me-"

"I learned how to give histamine injections so a man'll feel more pain. I learned about all kinds of drugs down there. I learned a human body's got a big nerve called the vagus that runs from your ass into your brain. That's important when you're making a man slide down a greased pole into his asshole by his own body weight. It takes fuckin' days that way. You should see their faces go through the changes."

"Calderone, you can have your revenge on me right now."

"I can do whatever I want," he said quietly. "I learned that in Mexico, too. No limits, man. No limits."

Suddenly, without even disturbing the air, he was next to me down on his haunches. He put the butterfly knife to my throat and lightly grazed the skin in a gentle sawing motion. "I got a long list of grievances to take up with you later. You thought I didn't know Marija was going to try to screw me out of the money."

"Let my wife go, Calderone," I begged.

"I took a hammer and found some German shepherd tied up behind his house and I beat that dog's skull in. I called your name every time I brought that hammer down on its fuckin' head."

"You can tear me up, anything."

"I got everything lined up in the basement and it's all for you, boy. Got me a nice set of shiny knives and some pliers. Got your garden hose down there, too. Even found me a jar of your wife's KY jelly. Most of all, I've got you, you piece of dog shit, and I've got time."

"You've got no time, Calderone. You need to take the money and run now!"

He stood up and touched my chin with his boot and raised my head to see him.

I lay my head down on the floor, exhausted from wheezing that out. My chest heaved with panic. I felt ice-cold fingers on my spine – my thoughts, my helplessness roosting in my cells. When you were drifting alone in the open sea, when you saw the first shark fins cut the surface, did it feel like this?

I heard his boots come off. One thud, two. A belt buckle jangled and made a different swooshing sound as it too hit the floor. Then I heard the zipper. He was at the first landing when he called down to me from the banister.

"Listen up real good, motherfucker, because I want you to hear every time she comes."

As he headed higher up the stairs, I heard him call her name; dread crawled like a tapeworm under my skin until my whole body shook on the floor. He said in a soft croon like children playing peek-a-boo: "Yoo-hoo, Sarah, up there, here I come...

"...and come... and come..."

SATURDAY, SEPTEMBER 11

12:01 A.M.

#40

In the bible, Judith cuts off the head of Holofernes after she wears him out in sex. The bloody-minded bible omits that part and lingers on the triumphal bloody head. I glimpsed Sarah's terrified face and I saw the courage she had in her, but I needed to see the guile of a woman who knew she had hours to live unless she found the courage to do what she never dreamed she'd have to do in a lifetime, let alone in the house where she felt safest.

While I lay on the floor with the dead eyes of Fat Boy staring into mine, I had nothing else to do but think. It wasn't lost on me that the gods were ladling out irony: what had Alicia's terror been, after all? I let rage percolate like oil under sand and waited for my mind to clear. It was still ricocheting like a ping pong ball in a room full of furniture – Montreal and the old terrors, Carlos, my escapades in the city, the face of my mother, all the chaos of the last two weeks.

Over the hours I lost all feeling in my hands, feet, and wrists; the numbness went all the way up my arms and only the shoulders felt the white-hot pain of my stretched-out tendons. My abdomen hurt and the tops of my thighs. Little by little, the pain censors were tripping or blinking out all over me. I tried to put my mind somewhere else by working variations of the Pythagorean formula and imagined myself sitting in a boat on Moose Lake with the sun casting shadows over different sides of my ball cap. I plotted the sun's azimuth by finding magnetic north to match the imagined landscape where Carlos and I had fished. I put an imaginary protractor on the angle between the shadow on my cap and the sun's position along the horizon to tell the time of day. You never know where your mind will take you in the moments before you're going to be killed.

The irony was that I heard nothing from upstairs. Not a sound. It wasn't possible for me not to in that quiet house beside a dead man. I heard cars start up in the distance as my neighbors awoke to begin a new work day. All was quiet above the stairs. I heard the creaks and tiny snaps a house makes on its own; her new ormolu clock on the fireplace mantle was making a deafening tock. Dogs woofed. I heard a squirrel in the red maple outside, but I couldn't hear Sarah being raped by a mad bull right over my head.

Fat Boy's boot knife...

I tried rocking. The pain was intense and I made no forward or backward progress from what I could see. I worked up a sweat and brought some deadened nerves back to flaming life; his middle-aged baby's face was right where it was when he fell, mocking me with slitted eyes that said: This ain't nothin'. Wait'll you see what he's gonna do to you. I resumed the rocking motion but all I was doing was creating intense pain and wearing myself out. With all my body weight centered, it wasn't possible. I was a turtle on its back. I had no other option but the faint hope Pippins would come knocking.

If you're ever thinking of being rescued, you've already lost. My father had a dozen sayings for this. I kept rocking, and after an hour, I made all of three inches' progress toward the corpse of Fat Boy. I was afraid of going into spasms at one point and the searing pain in every joint in my arms was unbearable. It felt like having my arms pulled behind me and being suspended in the air.

It seemed impossible but I was close enough to Fat Boy now to smell him. Not the rancid smell of his body but the overhanging smell of death. He was already showing dark patches of lividity on his face and arms. I changed the rhythm of my rocking to put as much torque as I could into the third swing. I gained a miniscule extra amount of ground that way even though the few feet separating us now seemed like the Alaskan tundra. I had sweated through my clothes and in one long exhausted spate where I couldn't move my body at all, I generated enough body heat to dry them.

Counting from the time I was brought in hog-tied and

dumped on the floor, I had spent hours working myself to exhaustion at this hopeless task. I was close enough to touch Fat Boy's cheek with my own. Once I had his body weight for leverage, however, I was going to be able to work more efficiently. It took me another forty-eight minutes to work down his body and angle myself so that my face was resting on his left leg. I had the sickening feeling that Calderone had removed the knife without my seeing it, and this was all for nothing.

His pant leg had to be pushed out of the way, and this was harder than I thought. I tried a hundred times to pull it back from his boot with my teeth. I failed every time.

I decided to eat my way through it. I began chewing at the edge where it was thickest. I tore at it like an animal in a leghold trap until my jaw ached. I had to stop and wait until my mouth could produce more spit. I did this for a long time with little to show for it but an abraded face and a dead man's slobbered boot. My lips were raw and bled. But it finally happened – a tiny rip.

I worked my way into the material with my face to get to the part where the material was like a tasteless pulp. I steadied myself and threw my head back with all my neck strength. I tore open a sore on the inside of my cheek but left no damage to the fabric. I worked my way back to it after worming and twisting over Fat Boy and prepared for the thrust. This time it was not going to fail, I said to myself. I thought of the basement. I thought of Sarah. Then I thought of Carlos. I snapped my head back and heard the satisfying rip of cloth.

I rested for ten minutes and then I began working toward the boot. Calderone had missed it because the sheath was made of very thin, supple leather. I used my teeth to loosen it inside the boot, and with my nose like a hog snout rooting for truffles, I managed to push it up his leg. It was like everything else so far: an upheaval of strain and agony for a millimeter of progress. I stopped checking the time but I knew hours were passing. The sun bloomed white through the backs of the heavy drapes Sarah installed.

I kept at it – a brainless, wriggling, six-foot worm of throbbing nerves and tortured muscles.

Then I had the knife in my teeth and I was able to extract it by the blade. The next part was worked out in my mind with angles. I couldn't get the blade near my hands, which were useless, so it was going to have to be feet first. I had to work the blade with my mouth so that I could stick it through the jelly of Fat Boy's eyeball and then drive it home into the brain's meat as far as I could manage. It took me awhile to get my legs in position so that I could create enough friction to cut into the cords at my feet. The knots weren't the problem. I had one cord to cut. I left about four inches of haft to work my leg against, abrading and sawing against thirteen pounds of head weight. Once I had worked my body up past his head and found the right angle where the tension on the nylon rope was greatest, it was a sawing action that required less strain on my upper body and my aching shoulders. Calderone and Fat Boy had figured on the knots as the important thing to hold me fast, but it was here that I had my only chance. I worked through the rest of the morning until it was the middle of the day.

Fear of Calderone tromping down the stairs in his biker

boots rarefied my hearing so much that I thought I heard the threads part. The weight of Fat Boy's head provided me all the ballast necessary to thrust and saw, thrust and saw...

I felt a last surge of adrenalin that gave me some release from the burning pain. I worked frantically until I felt the blade bite skin as well as cord. I didn't stop, I let the blood flow. It took my mind off the pain.

At last the rope parted and my legs swung loose. A loud sob escaped my throat. The realization I was unbound seemed like too much happiness. The sound of the bed bumping against the wall in the familiar rhythm of sex did something to my mind then. It wasn't the sound of rape I heard. It was the sound of a woman building up to climax.

I couldn't stand just yet even when I used the couch to help me get to a sitting position. The circulation in my legs was so bad that my thigh muscles fluttered uncontrollably. I sat there and breathed deeply, thinking of the exertions to come, and trying to hear and simultaneously block out the sounds from upstairs. The knife was almost corkscrewed into Fat Boy's socket and jutted out at a forty-five degree angle. I was going to have to sit on his head and work myself up and down from behind.

It would be easier than what I had just done, but I was too exhausted from the labor past to begin another task. I let precious seconds escape. I knew I could get out the door. My luck wasn't going to go on, and Calderone's lust would be sated eventually. I might make it to the street, but I'd be killed right there, and Sarah right afterward.

I went to work on my bindings and rode Fat Boy's head as if I were a buck scratching his behind against a tree. I worked and cut a few strands and rested. I heard Calderone in my mind telling her to do things and I heard her laugh and I wanted to ram my head into a wall to stop the sounds and the pictures in my brain.

It took another fifteen minutes to cut through and I didn't stop until I felt the warm blood pour down. I could not feel anything in my hands, but when my arms sagged free from their own weight, I thought this was like womb bliss. I had spent almost eight hours in and I was delirious and sick from the effort.

When I could stand up without falling over, I chafed my hands against anything I could to bring life back into them. When I had enough feeling in them to turn the door latch, I almost caved in to fear and bolted.

I breathed deeply and thought about what I was going to have to do. I put the filleting knife in my hands and squeezed them shut. It was the best I could manage. I started for the stairs.

I made it to the first landing on shaky legs and listened for sounds. Murmurs, low talk, post-coital noises of lovers – or so my mind let me think. I crept up the stairs and waited for the tell-tale creaks to bring a thundering reaction. Sarah laughed. It sobered me like stepping into a freezing mountain stream. I made my way down the darkened hallway to the bedroom; the door was opened and a puddle of yellow light spilled out.

Sounds became words and words became recognizable. Then bodies shifted on the bed, rustling sounds, and then slight slap of skin.

My consciousness was hearing Sarah's voice urge her demon lover on with words I knew – go deeper, fuck harder, fuck me, fuck me – and then cries of animal lust: oh, that's good, yes, yes, yes-

Whore, bitch.

I turned the corner and beheld them on the bed. Calderone was behind her pumping with his hands locked on her hips. His body dwarfed hers except for the rocking motion of the dirty bottoms of her feet sticking out from his thighs. Sweat rolled down his back. Fuck me, fuck me in the ass – oh, like that, like that, like that...

I was hallucinating, hearing the ghost in the machine, she was Marija, then she became herself again-

I walked right up to him and raised the knife. I lowered it. I was a foot from his neck. The commotion on the bed was building up and she was moaning even louder now for his cock, begging him to stick it all the way up her, harder, get his balls inside her if he could...

This is not going to sound like truth, but the next thing I remember was seeing the knife handle quivering in his back. He howled. He disengaged from her, but his erection had not gone flaccid. He tried to reach for the knife but it was too far down below his shoulder blade and stuck deep. When he turned to see who it was who had done this incredible thing to him, he roared and reached for my neck; he jerked me off the floor and flung me backward like a rag doll. He was on top of me throwing punches that flailed and missed my head and cracked the floor. He reared up with his hands locked into a single wrecking ball and brought them down on my chest. I thought my clavicle bone snapped. I almost blacked out from the pain.

Sarah hit him at a dead run from behind and rode his shoulders; she was screaming gibberish and biting his ear like an animal. With one hand, he pulled her by the hair down to his shoulder and threw an uppercut into her face – a straw-weight female taking on a super heavyweight. I was still stunned and lying helpless on the ground expecting any second for him to resume his pounding.

"Run!" I yelled.

Calderone's fist knocked my head sideways. My right eye swelled up and closed immediately. He drew his arm back for another punch but she hit him again just enough with her body to tilt his weight; he went down with her fingers gouging for his eyes in frenzy. Now there were two of us fighting him as well as a knife sticking in his back.

I threw a punch from the floor that didn't have much on it and sent an electric shock running up my arm. He turned back to face me. Sarah was a raging Furie, blood streaming down her face, fingers curled like talons aimed to rake Calderone's face. He fired shots that were glancing blows that hurt his hands more than my head. Sarah, free to move, had scooped up a lamp and was about to bring it down on the back of his head. That was enough to turn him toward her. I slid out from under his bulk while she distracted him with feints. Now we were at opposite ends, I was facing Calderone, negating his one-on-one power. Even his brute strength couldn't take us both down together in a heap.

"You fucker, I'll kill you!" Sarah screamed and lunged with the lamp.

"Sarah, no," I croaked. "Get... the Angel."

"What do you think you're gonna do, pussy," he sneered and drew himself up to size, relaxed, nimble on his feet again.

"You heard her. We... we're going to kill you, fucker," I said.

Calderone couldn't believe my audacity; he knew he was more than a match for four of us. But there was a hesitation in his voice, not so sure.

He did what I expected and came at me in a rush, a bull with a picador's shaft stuck in him. He slammed me backwards but I kept my feet moving at his speed and stayed upright as we hit the door. He threw a haymaker that would have finished me if I had stayed to receive it. Even with my bad eyes, I saw his telegraphed punches. Calderone was a bully, a street fighter, one of those loud shirt-ripping thugs who dominated by size. I threw a jab into his teeth that split open his lip. He roared and came at me again. I stepped sideways and hit him hard in the jaw with a right cross and a left to the kidneys – something I had done to my basement punching bag ten thousand times. Now I saw something else in his eyes: fear. It was a shot of adrenalin to my heart and I knew it wasn't going to be so big a mismatch, after all.

Meanwhile Sarah had armed herself with the Guardian Angel and was coming at him from behind. Time slowed to a glacier pace as I watched the clenched line of her jaw and the stringy sinews of her bicep as she slammed it into his back. Calderone wasn't fazed by the pain, but he was like a pit bull in a fighting ring snapping at everything that came close. He whipped a backhand out that connected with her arms and swept her aside like a cat swatting at a dust mote.

It was all the chance I might get if she was out of the fight. I lunged for the knife as I had once flung my whole body at Carlos' speeding car. I had both hands on the handle as I flew into him. I found leverage for a thrust just before his enormous strength bucked me off. Our legs tangled and we went down as he tried to twist away from the pain. He was losing his insane fury. It was a self-consuming fuel, useless to him. I was still holding on to the knife that was severing its way through his muscle. I kept twisting and leaning into it. Somehow, in a burst of strength from his big body, he shook me loose.

He staggered back to the window to take his bearings but flinging out his hand smashed the window and sliced open a cut that was deep and bled profusely. This was serious and he knew it. I could read his mind; the tide of battle had turned and he was going to need a gun to restore the balance he lost. He looked at me, bared his teeth, but said nothing. I held the knife in front of me and waited for the charge.

Calderone's chest was heaving hard. His face was a grim mask of pain. He had not expected any resistance, let alone a furious assault by a husband and wife he had dominated so easily. I was panting, too, but calm and a sense of control gave me legs to keep fighting. More than anything else, I knew I could not let him get to the guns he had stashed.

He lunged toward me, elbow up like a linebacker, in a feint that tried to bump me out of his way as he planted his foot and drove off it to my right. The old man's words never failed: attack the man, not the weapon. I switched the knife to my right hand and slashed out with it just as he drove past me toward the doorway.

I turned and watched him slam into the door and

bounce off it. He slapped a hand on to the red geyser spouting from his neck. He was out of sight in a second and running fast down the stairs.

I went over to Sarah and checked her pulse. She opened her eyes at my touch and started to fight me until she recognized me. Her nose was swollen and her eyes were tiny slits like a cat waking up.

"W-where is he? Jack, where did he go?"

"Easy," I said. "I'll take care of it."

"What are you saying? We have to call the police!"

"Look," I said and pointed at the floor where the door and ceiling had been spattered. She looked where I pointed at a small puddle of it.

"Blood," she said dully.

"His carotid."

"Help me up," she said.

"I'm going to finish it. He's not going to last more than a few minutes."

I didn't wait for her. I didn't think Calderone would have the skills to cinch off a spouting artery. While my mind was still clear, I was going to have to do it now or call the cops.

He was sitting in the kitchen slumped to the floor holding part of a cloth shirt to the gaping slash in his neck. It wasn't enough to stop him from bleeding out. The pools of red from the downstairs landing to the kitchen where he sat soaked in it looked like a red archipelago of islands linked by atolls and tidal reefs on a geological map. He looked up at me while his breath whistled through his teeth.

I looked down at him and tapped the knife against my

leg. "Don't waste your breath cursing me out," I said. I was shaking too hard to use the knife. I went out the door to the porch and grabbed hold of the bamboo chair to keep from collapsing. When I was steady enough, I went outside. The sun and the air almost induced a spasm of vomiting. I was wrapped in a stink of my own feral odor making me sicker. I walked down the driveway to the red stain, now a rusty brown patch in the grass. Ants were feasting on the dried stain in the driveway. I picked up the bat.

Hammerin' Hank Aaron. An old faded model with divots at the meat end and a big dent where some brown hairs had stuck to the splinters.

I walked back to the house dragging it through the grass.

Randall Calderone, Aryan Brother, convict and sometime skinhead, sat against the wall where I had left him. The gash in his hand was still leaking blood with his pumping heart, which was his real enemy now. His eyes were glazed like the eyes of a dying bird.

"Look at me," I said.

"Call... call ambulance," he said and coughed. He stared at me through glazed eyes in which the pupils were disappearing into the black.

"Look at me," I said. "This is for Carlos."

I swung the bat in a chopping downward stroke that connected with his head just above the right eye. It didn't break through the skull bone but it split the skin open. He said something that sounded like "Ugh," but he didn't move or try to ward off a blow.

"This is for Sarah," I said and swung again. The crunch

of skull was like a pistol shot.

"This is for me," I said and brought the bat down a third time. His bowels evacuated.

Whatever Calderone was in life, he had vacated the premises. I stepped back and focused on the spot where the skull cap is weakest and drew the bat back over my shoulder for another swing. This time the crunch was sufficient to tell me I had shattered more skull cap and bounced his brain around inside it.

It was like hitting a tree with an axe where the stroke isn't smooth and you get that ringing sensation clear to your elbow. The force knocked him sideways across the kitchen and he sprawled out like a body dumped from a moving car. His legs were crossed at the ankles and his arms extended out. I watched the blood flowing down his neck slow to a trickle and then the leak stopped altogether.

"Jack."

I turned to see Sarah staring at me. I didn't know how long she had been there.

"Jack," she said.

I held out my arms to her, but she pulled her bathrobe tighter across her and turned around. I watched her walk away and heard her go up the stairs. A few minutes later I heard the sirens screaming.

#41

I didn't know it then, but that would be the last time I would see my wife except for one other time when she came to court to testify at my trial. I don't count the two times she came to see me down in Orient at the Correctional Reception Center prior to my sentencing. I waited there in a holding pen for three months before transferring to the Ross Correctional Institute in Chillicothe at the southern end of the state. The guards were local, spoke with an accent, not like the flat Northern speech I was used to hearing since I had left Canada. Most were dyed-in-the-wool conservatives, believed in a mighty, wrathful God, and bragged about their sons and daughters who had served in Iraq or Afghanistan. When one of them came home in a silver casket, they would all line the streets waving tiny flags.

Several white buses were lined up the day we transferred from Columbus to take us to Lucasville, Mansfield, and Youngstown. Most of the men I rode with had done time before or were demoted back to maximum facilities for infractions in their medium-security prisons.

I remember the man next to me had body odor, how my breath steamed up the windows of the bus. It was a gray, cold day of icy sleet in late November. I was grateful the day was so bleak. It would have been much harder if the sun had been shining.

I still wake up from a bad dream once in a while. Mostly these are dreams where I'm suffocating – trapped in pipes or sewer drains. Like last night. I found myself trapped inside a tree – I was running from another one of those downpours that turned into a hail storm. Then a thunderstorm rolled in and lightning struck the ground everywhere. I climbed inside a hollowed-out tree and got stuck at the very moment I knew lightning would hit it. I worked my body past a family of possums so I wouldn't hurt them, and that's when I got good and stuck. I knew that fifty thousand volts would boil the sap so that the tree bark would explode. I could see my own pink viscera being blown outwards through the slits in the bark – it's like being instantly spaghettified by falling into the black hole of a collapsed star. In my disembodied mind, floating around like a green firefly, I see particles of guts like popcorn lying scattered across the ground. Then I see the wristwatch Sarah had given me, all dented and melted from the hot blast. I wake up with the aria of a scream still climbing out of my throat.

But everybody has dreams like that, right?

ABOUT THE AUTHOR

Robb White is the author of two hardboiled private-eye novels featuring his existentialist detective Thomas Haftmann, both published by Grand Mal Press: *Haftmann's Rules* (2011) and *Saraband for a Runaway* (2013). His crime novel *Special Collections* was the winner of the 2014 Electronic Book Series Competition by New Rivers Press. "Frotteur in the Dark" was selected by 10,000 Tons of Black Ink as one of 6 Best Of for 2009. That story was published in the collection *"Out of Breath" and Other Stories* by Red Giant Press of Cleveland in 2013. White also writes book reviews and does interviews for Tom Huff's magazine Boxing World.

ABOUT NUMBER THIRTEEN PRESS

PULP
CRIME
NOVELLAS

Number Thirteen Press is building a list of 13 quality crime novellas and short novels, to be published consecutively on the 13th of each month, from November 2014 to November 2015.

For all the latest info and to sign up for the newsletter, or for details about all 13 releases, go to www.numberthirteenpress.com

NUMBER THIRTEEN PRESS

#1 Of Blondes and Bullets – Michael Young
#2 Down Among the Dead – Steve Finbow
#3 The Mistake – Grant Nicol
#4 – When You Run with Wolves – Robert White
#5 - tba

www.numberthirteenpress.com

Printed in Great Britain
by Amazon